Henny and Lloyd, Private Eyes

Wings ePress, Inc.

Henny and Lloyd, Private Eyes

Some time passed, and our bank accounts dwindled, but on a Tuesday in November, one of Henny's fondest wishes came true. We sat at our desks, Henny reading *The Maltese Falcon* for what he swore was the eighth time, me wondering why Susan hadn't called. We'd seen each other at least once a week, and I'd phoned her each day since I'd seen her last, so I knew I'd held up my end of things.

You could sometimes fry eggs on the radiators in our office, so I'd cracked open one of the windows to relieve the desert atmosphere. Henny and I both heard them—two quick pops.

"Couldn't be," I chuckled. I don't particularly like the word 'chuckled.' Henny would say it certainly wasn't a word in the *noir* vocabulary. But, to be scrupulously accurate, I did chuckle. Henny went back to his book, and I returned to my stubborn cocoon of refusing to call Susan more than once a day. Soon, two dolorous knocks caused our heads to swivel toward our door. Henny tossed his book down and hurried to answer. He opened the door, and a woman, perhaps thirty or thirty-five years old, took two steps inside the office, dropped to her knees, and stared blankly at Henny before falling forward. From the noise her head made connecting...*bonk!*...with our wooden floor, I knew the worst had happened.

Henny and Lloyd, Private Eyes

John Paulits

A Wings ePress, Inc.
Mystery/Humor Novel

Wings ePress, Inc.

Edited by: Christie Kraemer
Copy Edited by: Jeanne Smith
Executive Editor: Jeanne Smith
Cover Artist: Richard Stroud

Wings ePress Books
www. wings-epress.com

Copyright © 2018 by John Paulits
ISBN 978-1-61309-665-9

ublished In the United States Of America

Wings ePress Inc.
3000 N. Rock Road
Newton, KS   67114

What They Are Saying About
Henny and Lloyd

"Henny and Lloyd are two of the sharpest-drawn, and funniest, characters in all of detective fiction, in my view, and as a man with a library of several hundred examples of such fiction, I've met quite a few. Their talents for solving crime are not bad either."

—Kirkpatrick Sale, author of *Human Scale, Revisited*

"These stories are both humorous and interesting. The Philly police could have used sharp minds like Henny's and Lloyd's on the force. Michael Connelly, don't look back. Here comes John Paulits, the new king of suspense. Looking forward to more stories."

—Bob Swierczewski, Philadelphia Police Lieutenant (Ret.)

Dedication

For Timmi and Tiger

One

Henny and Lloyd's First Case

It was the dawn of a new era, and I felt proud as I stood across the street from the old New York City factory building where Henny and I had rented an office. There in a third-floor window sat our sign, lettered and painted by our own little hands on a big piece of white poster board, after we'd priced neon, proclaiming HENNY AND LLOYD—PRIVATE DETECTIVES. In smaller letters, it read Third Floor—just in case clients were so overwrought with their problems they couldn't count up to our window. The building rose above us, floors four through ten, filled with city offices, and from a seventh-floor window, Mayor de Blasio's face smiled upon the neighborhood from what looked like an election poster. Henny's face appeared above our sign. He waved me upstairs. I waved back but looked around before moving, taking in the historic—to me—moment.

We'd chosen an office in this building because it came cheap. And besides, it put us only a few blocks from Chinatown and across the street from Napoli Pizzeria, so an inexpensive lunch—the only kind Henny and I ate—would be easy to find.

Our office had only one double window, but fortunately the buildings across the street were low enough to allow the sun to shine in when the planets aligned properly. The sign in the window one office over from us read ECHOE LIGHTING COMPANY. The lighting company rented the corner space in the building and had signs in windows facing both Centre and Grand Streets. In neon. Diagonally across the street was the old police headquarters. A new HQ had been in operation down by the Brooklyn Bridge for years, and the old one turned into zillion-dollar condos, although why anyone would buy a zillion-dollar condo in this ten-cent neighborhood befuddled me.

I crossed the street and walked into the filthy lobby of our building. The original white marble walls were yellowed and graffiti-covered now, and the floor had a gap-toothed, white mosaic design. One look at the elevator, which had no hint of either expedition or safety to it, would send any sensible person five feet over to the open doorway of the pungently aromatic stairway. That's where I headed. If I were to die on the job, I didn't want it to be from an elevator mishap. I took a deep breath and dashed up the two flights of stairs to our office. Painted on our frosted office door window were the same words as on our window sign, less the reminder about the third floor. I looked proudly at our names and thought of the scene in *The*

Maltese Falcon where Bogie tells his secretary to get the window and door repainted and have Miles Archer's name removed. Henny and I pretended to worry about which of us would be the one to give a similar order to our secretary. If we ever got a secretary. If we ever got a case.

I opened the door and there sat Henny, feet up on one of the two old, scarred, wooden desks we found in a junk store on Lafayette Street, a couple of blocks away.

"This is living," he said. "We finally did it. P. I.s. Look in your bottom drawer."

I sat at the other desk, our windows behind me, and opened the bottom drawer. A bottle of Boone's That's All whisky nestled there.

"Where'd this come from?"

"I bought it. Where do you think it came from? A bon voyage present for both of us as we set sail on a sea of crime. Marlowe and Spade each kept a bottle in the office. It's good for the image. Pour us a drink."

"Now? Into what?" I asked, looking over the spare office.

"Here's a little trick I know." Henny took a plain piece of printer paper from our printer tray and rolled it into a funnel. "Pour."

"Into that? It'll go all over the floor," I protested.

Henny got up and walked over to my desk. He took the bottle, which I'd opened, and poured some into the paper. He held it up to me to show nothing coming out of the bottom. Then he tossed back the drink.

"Do one for me," I said.

He did, and I drank from it, marveling at my clever partner and wondering what the hell I was doing drinking Boone's That's All at eleven o'clock in the morning.

"We're not having this for breakfast every morning, are we?" I asked Henny.

"Setting a tone today." He leaned back and replaced his feet on the desk. I did the same. Today, this glorious first day on the job, was not a day to be picky. Henny and I were licensed detectives, private investigators. Cool, tough dicks. I remember telling my dad, when I was fourteen or fifteen and under the spell of Bogie and Spade and Marlowe, that I wanted to be a dick when I grew up. He nodded wearily and told me the only way I'd ever be a dick was if I changed my name to Richard. I realize now he could've said worse. Well, I'm still Lloyd, not Richard, and damned if I'm not a dick anyway. And at twenty-five years old, too. Ah, if only all of Henny's and my future days could feel as promising and pleasant as this one.

They didn't. A week dragged by as we waited for a client, one client, to knock on our door. We didn't want to be out of the office and maybe miss a call, so it became a big treat when my turn came to walk to Chinatown and bring back lunch. When neither of us wanted the long walk, we lunched on pizza from across the street. With all the garlic Henny and I used, we could've done a hell of a business putting vampires in their place. Good thing we didn't need to kiss our clients to get their cases. If we ever got any clients. Henny wondered out loud whether we'd picked the best spot for our office. It seemed we'd chosen the one crime-free neighborhood in New York City.

"Of course we didn't," I reminded him. "We picked a dump we could afford."

Our meager online presence hadn't yet gone viral—hadn't even caught a cold, actually—and the only advertising we'd done, besides our window sign, was to put fliers under the windshield wipers of parked cars in the neighborhood when we went out for pizza. We'd already found twenty two of those balled up and tossed in front of our office door. And so, we waited.

We waited, and we read. Mystery stories, naturally. We planned to deduct the used paperbacks on our tax return as a business expense. If we ever had any income. Henny went for the hard-boiled Marlowe and Spade types. I leaned to the softer variety with a dandy puzzle, ala Ellery Queen and good old Sherlock. We were sitting in the office on our second Monday in business, quietly reading, when that most glorious of sounds reached our ears. A knock on the door.

Henny and I looked over our books at each other.

"Did you hear something?" Henny asked.

The knock came again.

"What do we do?" Henny whispered. "Should I get out my gun?"

I gave him a "don't-be-dumb" look and tossed my book down. "You're closer. Answer it."

Henny stood and stepped toward the door. Before he opened it, he dashed back to his desk and took a toothpick from a box in the top right-hand drawer. He slid the toothpick into the left side of his mouth and amended his walk to a swagger. I hated it when Henny started with his toothpicks, but we had no time to discuss it now. Henny opened the door to a woman, a distraught woman, who looked to be in her forties. Early forties. A woman who'd seen better times. She had a dark blue handkerchief in her hand, and a damned big one it was. She kept dabbing her eyes with it and sniffing prodigiously. Her hair was blonde and seemed to be glued in place. Not a hair moved, not a hair in disarray. Her clothes were not stylish; downright frumpy, actually. She wore a blue suit, the skirt of which swished to an end near her ankles. Her white blouse sported an enormous bow, behind which her chin disappeared whenever she opened her mouth to talk. She wore shoes with sensible low heels and a little pillbox hat, the Jackie Kennedy style which I hadn't seen in I don't know how long. She lifted her eyes from her handkerchief and looked at us. Her makeup, heavily packed on, hadn't smeared. Fighting off the ravages of time, I supposed. Heck of a way to try to look young, though, by calling attention to the losing battle you were fighting to do so.

But she was a client and, in our eyes, beautiful.

She stood in the doorway looking back and forth between Henny and me until Henny offered her our client chair, an old wooden thing with wheels some ancient elementary school teacher once rolled across the floor in. As he went through the necessary introductions, I couldn't help noticing how the harsh light from the window behind me streamed over our prospective client and highlighted her every facial flaw. Illumination was not her best friend. Her makeup struck me again. The image of a plumber caulking her furrows rose in my mind. Hell, I'd rather've been old with no makeup than covered with the goop she'd put on. But, of course, I'm not a woman; nor am I old. Henny invited her to state her case, so I got out a pad of paper. Notes were important. Or so they'd told us in online detective school.

"It's my daughter, Mr. Henny, Mr. Lloyd."

Henny and Lloyd were our first names, but she could call us anything she wanted.

"She's getting married Saturday, and I want to keep her from committing the gravest mistake of her life."

"Who's she marrying, ma'am?" asked Henny, rolling his toothpick to the right side of his mouth. I wished he'd throw the stupid thing away. He looked ridiculous.

"The man's name is Raymond. Giles Raymond. My daughter is Geeta Daniels, Margarita, actually. Geeta's a nickname. I'm Mrs. Marion Daniels. My husband died five years ago. So I'm responsible…responsible for Geeta's happiness." She began sniffing and dabbing with the big blue handkerchief again. I felt a wave of elation, realizing our very first case had this delicious spark of romantic, family drama to it. A crying client and a dastardly groom-to-be. A detective couldn't ask for more.

"We understand," Henny said as I wrote down all the names and relationships on my pad. "What would you like us to do? What's the problem?"

"Geeta wants to marry Giles, and I know he's merely using her. I know he sees other women. I know he's a two-timer, a four-flusher."

I saw Henny perk up. Four-flusher was one of his favorite 1940s' detective expressions. I didn't know exactly what it meant—you had to have five for a flush, didn't you?—but when Mrs. Daniels mentioned it, I supposed she meant someone who didn't have all the goods but liked to portray himself as having them.

"How do you know?" Henny asked.

"I know this man. I hear from others. I once followed him myself to see where he went." Her voice softened as if ashamed of her behavior. "I know where he goes, and I tell my daughter all about him, but she doesn't believe me, of course. He's convinced her he loves her."

"You tailed him, eh?" Henny switched his toothpick left to add some gravitas to his pronouncement. "Where did he go?"

"To see other women, of course!" she answered, as if the answer should be obvious. Especially to two trained, top notch detectives.

I tried a better question. "Why would he be using your daughter? What would he get out of it? Besides your daughter, I mean."

"Money. When my daughter marries, she will come into the money her father put away for her."

"How much?" I asked.

She took the blue handkerchief away, sniffed and said, "Five hundred thousand dollars."

Sheesh! I'd've married the mother for half that.

"Good reason," said Henny as the toothpick slid to the right. "You want us to tail this Giles Raymond and get the goods on him?"

I shot Henny a look. Toothpick. Tailed. Get the goods. The guy lived in the forties and loved his work.

"If my daughter doesn't believe me, she'll have to believe two private detectives. I want you to follow him, watch his house, take pictures of the women he sees, the women who see him, and get this report to me by Friday morning. Can you do it?"

The way she put it sounded like a high school pep rally. Can you do it? Go team! Go! Go!

Henny nodded with enthusiasm. "We'll need addresses and his daily schedule, where he works, photos of him. You give us that, we'll go to work."

Mrs. Daniels pulled a manila envelope from her large handbag and dropped it in front of Henny. "You charge a fee, no doubt?"

I cleared my throat. "We do."

Henny jumped in. "You'll want both of us on this case, I'm sure."

"Oh, yes. It's so important."

"Then we'll have to ask five hundred dollars a day. Plus expenses."

I looked at Henny and, as Mrs. Daniels fished in her purse, mouthed the words, "Five hundred!"

"Fine," said Mrs. Daniels, extracting her checkbook. She wrote out a check, and Henny and I reached out for it when she finished. I shot Henny another look, and he settled back into his chair and got out a new toothpick. Henny didn't have a head for figures. We'd already agreed I'd take care of the money. I looked at the check, and as Mrs. Daniels replaced her checkbook in her purse, I held up two fingers to Henny and mouthed the words, "Two thousand." Henny puffed out his cheeks. Two months' rent on this dump! I had to turn the two fingers I'd raised into a brush of my hair when Mrs. Daniels looked my way and provided the info we needed. After reminding us she needed results by Friday, the day before the wedding, she left, pressing the big blue handkerchief to her eyes.

Henny put his finger to his lips, and we waited until we heard the elevator doors open and close, and the elevator begin its creaking journey to the ground floor. Henny leaped up and stood on top of his desk. "We're in the chips, Lloyd. This is only the beginning. Nothing's gonna stop us now. Let's go follow our Floyd Thursby." He leaped from his desk, and I followed him out the door.

We were back in the office twenty seconds later.

"I was following you, Henny. Why ask me where we're going? Where did you think you were going?"

"It seemed the right thing to do. Get to work right away."

"Sheesh! You got us charging out the door without knowing where we're going. The guy's at work now, for Pete's sake. Look, I'm going to the bank and deposit this little beauty. You stay here. Study what's in the envelope she gave us. When I get back, we'll approach this case with some intelligence. If you have any. Jesus, rushing out the door to nowhere."

"I have intelligence, plenty of it. Just hurry back."

Two

The info inside the manila envelope informed us that Giles Raymond was a big deal securities salesman with Schlemer, Schlemer, Schlemer, and McCormick, office at 85 Broad Street, a monster of a building across the street from the Fraunces Tavern, where George Washington said farewell to his assistants after the Revolutionary War ended. Raymond didn't look much like a wheeler-dealer or philanderer in the photo Mrs. D. gave us. Actually, he looked like a dweeb, a dork. A poor man's Wally Cox or maybe even Arnold Stang, if anybody remembers them. Hardly the type to be the playboy Ms. D. suspected. But here I stood, lurking outside the main entrance of 85 Broad Street. Henny had gone off to lurk outside the brownstone Raymond owned on Leroy Street. Owning a brownstone meant he did pretty well with his securities.

Anyway, I was to tail Raymond when he left work and meet Henny on Leroy Street. Or call Henny to join me if Raymond didn't go home. Or join Henny if I missed Raymond, and he went home. We had it all worked out. According to Ms. D., he left work around six, but when six forty-five came, and still no Raymond, I put my brain to work. This was where I excelled Henny. I enjoyed the puzzle. I loved the figuring-out part. Henny saw himself as our street operative. The question: Did I miss Raymond leaving or was he still in the building? I had the answer. I whipped out my cell and called Raymond on the office number Ms. D. had given us. Whoever answered told me I'd missed Raymond by minutes, so I huddled behind my tree and, sure enough, a moment later, Raymond, dressed in a dark blue suit and carrying a brown briefcase, walked out of the building. This was my first head-to-toe look at the man. I'd've been shocked if he tipped the scales at more than one hundred twenty-five pounds. There wasn't much to this guy, plus he was bald in the bony way emaciated men get. Little tufts of side hair waggled over his ears, but not so much as one strand covered his dome. Not much of a physical attraction for the daughter to latch onto. He hailed a cab.

"Nuts," I muttered. Raymond got in, and the cab immediately got caught at a red light. I grabbed the next cab. "Can you stay behind the cab in front of us?" I asked excitedly. Henny would've said, "Follow that cab."

"Are you for real?" asked Abdul Serhakkian, my driver.

The light turned green, and I ripped my wallet from my pants pocket. I flashed my detective license and said, "Police work."

"Police work. Big deal," Abdul mumbled, but he pulled out after the cab.

Raymond went straight home to Leroy Street. I paid my fare and wrote down the amount in my notebook, the first recorded expense in the history of the Henny and Lloyd Detective Agency.

Another proud moment. I might even frame it. Raymond climbed the stoop to his front door and went inside.

Leroy Street is a spectacular street. At least the block between Varick and Hudson Streets. Old brownstones lined one side of the block, a dozen of them. They leapt out at the eye because, walking from Varick Street, you passed two wide, five-story tenements from the 1920s. You expected very little from the street at this point. But across from the big blue flag proclaiming the Hudson Park Branch of the New York City Library, Leroy Street swerved. You passed from the shadow caused by the bulky library building into the sunlight let into the block by the wide-open playground of the Carmine Street Recreation Center. There, what you hadn't seen before were those dozen glorious brownstones, all the same height, the middle nine the same design. Splashes of greenery, small trees, bushes, and some ivy enlivened the tiny cement-covered yards in front of each house. Trees lined both sides of the street.

Raymond lived in a gray-painted building near the middle of the line of houses, the only light-colored front in the lot. "Eleven," the front door proclaimed. The house had a ground floor and three upper floors. Henny popped up at my shoulder.

"He came right home from work," I said. "Now what?"

Henny's eyes glowed in ecstasy. "We watch. This is the glamour part of our chosen profession. A stakeout."

I didn't see much glamor in a stakeout, but Henny really bought into it. We watched but not for long. It was still light, nearly seven-thirty, when a woman came down the street. I said a quick prayer. Please be heading to Raymond's place.

"Get your camera out, Henny," I whispered excitedly. "Get it ready." Henny got ready.

"I wonder if she's the real girlfriend," I said. "The daughter Geeta."

Henny tapped my pocket. I pulled out the photos Ms. D. had given us and studied the photo of Geeta. No, not close. I showed it to Henny. He shook his head.

"The hair," he said. "All wrong."

Geeta was a smiling brunette. The woman approaching was a somber blonde. I tapped Henny's camera, and he attached the fancy lens he used for long distance work and began snapping.

"The lens cover," I said. "Get it off. Get it off."

Henny snatched off the black plastic cover and managed to shoot a couple more shots as the young woman paused a moment and looked back toward the street. I nudged Henny to keep snapping. The woman took out a key and let herself into the house, using the ground floor entrance rather than climbing the short flight of stone steps to the more elegant first floor entrance Raymond used.

"Entering slyly, like a mistress," Henny said to me.

"Let me write it all down," I said. "Tell me what you saw."

"Young woman. Blue dress. Blonde hair. Stylish. Carrying a large leather bag. High-heeled shoes. She arrived at seven-twenty and let herself into Raymond's house—ground floor—with her own key. Raymond lives alone so she must be there to see him. I think we have something, Lloyd."

"If you got the lens cap off in time."

"First case jitters. Don't worry about it. We have to stay and see what time she comes out."

I frowned. "Henny, she could be there all night."

"All the better. She's an illicit girlfriend. The longer she stays, the more incriminating. We have to know."

"We, as in both of us?"

"All right. All right. One of us can do it. We'll take turns. I'll flip you for who goes first. Winner stays."

"Heads," I said. Heads came up, and Henny started off smiling. "I'll relieve you in three hours. If she comes out early, I'll be at Walkers. Call."

Walkers was a neighborhood bar a half-mile south of us—a ten-minute walk. I nodded glumly as Henny strode away.

It was a few minutes before ten when the woman left Raymond's house, again like a thief in the night, through the ground floor entrance. She checked up and down the street and even looked my way. From where I stood behind a tree, the woman looked pretty good. Raymond must have some personality. The woman walked away from me toward Hudson Street. I waited until she turned the corner and, after duly noting her departure time, headed for Walkers, another cab ride I'd charge to Ms. D.

Every night afterward, I followed Raymond home from work and met Henny on Leroy Street. Every night around seven thirty, a different woman carrying a different large, leather bag would arrive, sometimes coming from Varick Street, sometimes from Hudson Street. The woman would stop and look around suspiciously before slipping quietly into the house through the ground floor entrance. Always with her own key. Ms. D. sure had him pegged. Raymond was proving to be a world-class juggler of women. I grew a tad jealous of Giles Raymond's way with women and told Henny so as we sat in the office Friday morning after sending our report of Raymond's four active nights, along with the photos corroborating them, to Ms. D. as requested.

"Well," said Henny. "Two blondes, a redhead, one with black hair. It took a lot of standing around (we'd each stood watch two nights), but our first case is over. We did the job. We earned the two thousand bucks. Now, all we have to do is wait for another client."

"Oh, is that all?" I asked.

Late Friday afternoon, a rapid knocking tattooed our office door. Henny's eyebrows lifted. He grabbed a toothpick and went to answer. A young brunette, in tears, rushed into the room. I recognized her from our photo collection. Geeta Daniels. Behind her, like a tiny canoe caught in the wake of a mighty ocean liner, puttered Giles Raymond.

"Are you responsible for this?" she cried and threw our report on my desk.

"Yes," I said. "We're Henny and Lloyd."

"That's our work," Henny said coolly.

"How could you send my mother such horrible lies?"

"They're not lies, ma'am," I said. "They are the result of professional detective work."

"Lies, lies, lies. Tell them, Gilly."

Henny and I exchanged a glance. Gilly?

"Oh, yes, yes. Lies. I know none of these women…"

"See," said Geeta. "Gilly swears this report is full of lies. Tell them what you did all last week, Gilly."

"I spent every night last week with you, dear. You came…"

"See," Geeta cut in. "My mother paid you to fabricate rubbish like this, so she could try to trick me, intimidate me. She doesn't want me to see Gilly any more. That's it, isn't it? Admit it."

"No," said Henny, lines appearing between his eyes. "We took those pictures outside of Mr. Raymond's house on Leroy Street."

"Oh, do you hear what they've told Mother, Gilly? The lies they've told her? She said this morning I must break off with you. What shall we do?"

Gilly, I mean Giles, took out a handkerchief, a white one, and mopped his forehead. A day at the securities' desk must never have been like this. "I don't know, darling. You know how much I love you."

"Mother doesn't believe it. You've been telling me you love me for almost a year. I know you love me, but now Mother insists she has proof you don't! She has these photos, Gilly. Oh, these women, these women. It's not true, is it?"

"But darling, I…I was with…"

"Oh, these photographs, Gilly."

"…you. I don't understand."

"Mother was wild, absolutely wild, when she tossed them at me this morning. Actually gloating! She believes these photos, Gilly, and I can't, I simply can't, marry against my mother's will." Softly, she added, "You know I love her, too, darling." She ratcheted up the volume and went on. "Oh, if there were only some way to prove to my mother how much you love me, Gilly. You do love me, don't you, Gilly?"

"Well, of course I do. We could…I mean…it is sudden, but I mean we could…it's always possible…"

"What is, Gilly? What is? Think of a way, darling."

"You have…you did have us get the license in case we ever should decide to… you know…decide to…" Gilly swallowed prodigiously.

"Mother will be waiting at home for us. She'll insist we never see each other again. Oh, these damnable photos. If only we were married already."

"We…we…could get…m…married, I suppose. I mean, if you think that would convince her. I mean…" Raymond shrugged.

"Oh, darling Gilly. How could it not convince her? Yes, I do have our license with me." And Geeta threw herself into Gilly's arms and plastered his mouth with a kiss. She pulled back and smiled into the little man's face.

"Today. Let's get married today, Gilly. Let's go home as man and wife. It will prove to Mother how much you love me. Mother will be so happy."

"Whatever you think best, dear." Gilly wiped his forehead again and looked as if the firing squad leader had shouted out, "Ready…aim…"

"Let me go and clean my face and we'll go down to City Hall. It's walking distance from here, isn't it, Mr. Henny?"

She looked at me. "Yes, straight down Centre Street to the Municipal Building. Walk it in about fifteen minutes. Nice day outside."

"Ladies room?" she asked.

"Down the hall to the left," I directed.

"I won't be long, Gilly darling." Geeta swept out of the room.

Gilly darling joined Henny and me in a profound silence.

Henny looked puzzled and asked, "I'm sorry. Weren't you and the young lady already planning to get married? Tomorrow, I'd heard."

"Married! Oh, no. Oh, my. Tomorrow? No. I have a dental appointment tomorrow. Married, no. Had a near heart attack when Geeta suggested getting a license just in case. No, not until this very minute," he stopped to wipe his brow—'Fire!'— "did I know I'd be getting married."

Henny looked my way. "So, go to work, Mr. Puzzle," he said.

"Have you met Geeta's mother?" I asked.

"Once, about six months ago. A gray-haired, elderly, most refined woman. Sweet. But from the stories Geeta tells me, a she-dragon, a gorgon, gentlemen. I've grown deathly afraid of her. To tell the truth, I have. You heard. She's a suspicious beast."

I continued my interrogation. "Elderly, you say? Around, what? Forty?"

"Forty! Oh, no. More like sixty. At least sixty."

I looked at Henny.

"And the inheritance?"

"Inheritance? Who died?" Gilly asked.

"Her father?"

"No, no. Hale and hearty. Fine gentleman. Wouldn't be an inheritance if he did die. They're quite poor, you know. Feel sorry for him, married to the gorgon. Can't understand how the mother could have changed so from when I first met her."

"Does Miss Daniels work?" I asked.

"Teaches kindergarten. Hates the little monsters."

The door opened, and Geeta returned, all smiles. "I'm so happy, darling. I really am."

"Happy, yes…ah, yes, me, too." Gilly's facial expression came well short of confirming his words. He wiped his forehead again.

"Mother will be so pleased," Geeta repeated, and she began to cry. "Come, my darling." And she led little Gilly from the office. In no time, she re-entered, alone, still teary-eyed.

"Let me give you this," she said. "So there will be no trouble. Say no more about any of this."

She placed a check on my desk. I looked at it. Another thousand dollars.

"Oh," she said, full of emotion. "You two gentlemen have helped make me the happiest girl on earth." She began blubbering again and pulled an enormous blue handkerchief from her purse. Henny and I had seen the handkerchief before. Geeta Daniels closed the door behind her.

Henny and I sat immobile, too embarrassed to look at one another.

Finally, I picked up the check Geeta had laid on my desk. "It has M. Daniels printed on it. Same as the first one. She's the M. Daniels on the check. Margarita," I said. "Not her mother, Marion."

"She was all the women?" asked Henny. "She was all the women! And the mother? Is that possible?"

"Sure. Why not? The big leather bags those women carried had her implements in them. No wonder she used the downstairs entrance. She needed time to change into and out of her disguise without Gilly catching on."

"And we watched her force the poor schmuck to marry her," said Henny. "Right here in this office! Maybe we should've started a lonely hearts online dating service instead of a detective agency."

"He's the one with the dough, not her," I said. "I don't feel well. We deserve to have both our names taken off the door."

Henny's head sank. "The bottom drawer of your desk, please."

I pulled out the bottle of Boone's That's All, while Henny folded two pieces of printer paper. He held them while I poured.

"To better times, Henny," I toasted.

We drank. Then we drank again.

Three

The Election

After a dismal weekend, Henny and I had a dismal week, followed by another dismal weekend. Neither one of us brought up the Geeta Daniels case. No one knocked on our door. No one called us on the phone. No one sent us a desperate email, begging for top-flight detective services. I found even more of our windshield fliers crumpled up and tossed in front of our office door. Those things cost money, you know. Henny put aside his fantasies about detective life in the 1940s and substituted fantasies about Depression life in the 1930s. We read our paperbacks, and we ate our pizza. I finished my book, John Dickson Carr's, *The Three Coffins*, at my desk on Monday morning and went out for a *NY Post*. The primary election season for local governmental seats was in full swing, and a news story today highlighted the contest between two neophyte, local candidates vying for a seat on the city council to replace the incumbent, who'd received a promotion to a jail cell upstate for a two-year term, where he could sit and contemplate the error of his ways as well as plan how to spend the money he'd stolen when he ultimately went free.

Both candidates were Democrats—it being a primary election. Whoever won would have no opposition in November, Republicans having a snowball's chance in hell for anything elective in New York City. The primary mattered.

Prudence Holiman had a pedigree teeming with concerned community involvement—food banks, dental care for the elderly, nutritious school lunches. Stuff like that. Her opponent, Randolph Miserly, was an older fellow who'd made a boatload of money in NYC real estate. His spiel centered on his nascent desire to give back to the community after his lifetime of financial success.

The page four story in the day's *Post* ran under the headline: "Holiman Accuses Miserly of Colluding with Real Estate Interests."

"Henny," I called over to the other desk. "You ever colluded?" I suppose I felt giddy from the lack of work.

"What? What are you talking about?" Henny tossed his paperback onto the desk. "I'm bored. So bored, maybe I'll try colluding. What is it?"

"I asked you."

We stared at each other.

"It's in the story here." I tapped the paper.

"Read me the story."

The story documented an allegation from the Holiman camp that Mr. Miserly was in cahoots with the real estate lobby, which had its eye on a stretch of tenement buildings on Mulberry Street in Little Italy. The block went so: the ten buildings, from the 1890s or earlier, in question—if you saw *The Godfather, Part II*, the De Niro part, you'll have the area pictured—a parking lot, then similar buildings the rest of the block. The article mentioned a fellow named David Toledo, a prominent real estate magnate, who wanted the ten buildings condemned and knocked down to make room for a glorious new apartment building complex with equally glorious high rents. The high rent part I assumed. Miserly swore up and down, though he and Toledo worked together in the past, he, Miserly, was committed to his newly-won, community-oriented, voter-friendly sensibilities and would do nothing to hurt the community. With her do-gooder history, Prudence Holiman's affection for, and loyalty to, the tenants of the buildings under discussion went unchallenged. Those people, she claimed, some of whom had lived there for over sixty years with their grandparents living there before them, were a priority of hers. Nothing in the article disputed Prudence's purity on the topic.

I knew for a fact City Council members were notoriously courteous to one another over issues which involved only their own district. No one wanted to be told no by the other council members in such a case, so, usually, no one said no. Live and let live. The fear was, if Randolph Miserly won the city council seat, it would seal the deal with David Toledo, everyone's denials notwithstanding. Out with the old (buildings); in with the new (giant building).

"So colluding means working together?" Henny pondered. "I collude with you."

"We haven't colluded lately," I pointed out.

"We colluded two weeks ago."

"Right. How'd that turn out?"

"Paid the rent. Keeps us in pizza. Seems we gotta learn to collude better."

I sighed and closed the newspaper. The moment I did so, a knock sounded on our door, three thumps, and Henny grabbed for a toothpick.

"You sit," I told him. His toothpick hadn't betokened much luck last time. "I'll get it." A short, wide gentleman in a pin-striped suit stood framed in the doorway. He wore a fedora. I heard of moan of pleasure behind me and knew Henny had seen the fedora and already pictured the office going black and white with Bogart or Bacall following the man inside. None of that happened, other than the man's coming inside.

"How do you do, sir?" I offered and gestured him to our client chair. "I'm Lloyd and this is Henny." Henny rose to shake the man's hand, but as Henny ascended, the man descended, and no handshake occurred. The man waited for me to find my chair as well. I did and asked how we could help.

"Yous are aware, I'm sure, of a upcoming city council election happening in this neighborhood, are you not?"

I opened my newspaper to page four and held it in front of him. "We were discussing it before you came in. Interesting story."

"I am representing a certain candidate."

When he said "certain," he said "soitain."

"May I ask which one?" Henny asked.

"When I explain my purpose, you'll know which one."

When he said "purpose," he said "poipose."

"Please explain your poi…er…purpose," Henny said.

"There is a important issue in this election."

When he said "there" and "this," he said "dare" and "dis." You can figure it out from here.

"I'm sure there are many," Henny inserted.

The man glared at him. "There's one."

"Yes, of course," I interrupted. "One. Please, go on. Oh, may I know your name?"

"You can call me Smith. Mr. Smith."

"Yes, Mr. Smith, go on," I repeated.

"You know that crook Miserly says he wants to preserve a very historic row of old buildings on Mulberry Street, but we think different. We think he's in bed with the real estate interests and plans to throw out those sweet families what been living there for generations. If those buildings go, so goes history. You know what I mean? Living there generations!"

Mr. Smith's eyes rolled up and his lips moved as if he were trying to remember the next lines of his part in a play.

"Wait a minute...generations," he repeated. "This Holiman lady wants to preserve the historic block and keep those families in their childhood." A look of confusion swept over Mr. Smith's face. "I mean in their childhood homes. Childhood homes." He nodded in satisfaction. "That's where yous come in."

Henny and I waited, but no explanation issued forth from Mr. Smith.

"Yes," Henny said, breaking the tension. "We come in...?"

"Yes, yous come in and..." Mr. Smith's eyes narrowed as he concentrated. In a soft voice he said, "Uh, yous come in and...and... Oh! yeah, this is where yous come into the picture. We don't want the bum Miserly to win. Yous guys gotta dig up some dirt we can use against him in the election, and there ain't much time. You any good at that?"

"Good!" Henny blurted. "We're better than good. We're the best."

"You better be."

My stomach did a fancy dance step.

"So you know," Mr. Smith went on. "I was never here. Yous two never seen me. You copacetic with that?"

I knew Henny had no idea what copacetic meant because I didn't know what it meant, but Henny said we were copacetic, and I couldn't have been more copacetic if I tried.

"I got a name to give you, but don't stop there. You dig. I wanna know Miserly stole a nickel from his kindergarten teacher. I wanna know he stole a Hershey Bar from the candy store. I wanna know he cheated on a spelling test. I wanna know he cheated on his wife. I wanna know he skipped out on his taxes. I wanna know he hates cripples. I wanna know he hates brown people. The vote's in eight days. I wanna know…everything!" Mr. Smith voice rose as he made his way through the litany of items he wanted to know. "I make myself clear?"

"Very," both Henny and I said, stumbling over one another to answer first.

"Here's a name." He tossed a small brown bag onto my desk. I could see money in it. I picked up the edge of the bag and looked more closely.

"Uh, Benjamin Franklin?"

"What? What do you mean Benjamin Franklin?"

"Benjamin Franklin's the only name in the bag," I pointed out.

"What? Huh? Oh. What'd I do? Yeah, that's your fee. Could be more later, you dig real good."

"I dig real good, man," Henny assured Mr. Smith, adding a circle made with his index finger and thumb.

"Uh, Henny," I muttered. "I don't think that's what he means."

"You worked with this guy very long?" Mr. Smith asked, dubiousness dripping from this tone.

"He's my top man," I assured Mr. Smith. Mr. Smith did not look assured, but he moved on.

"I'll be visiting here on occasion for news. Don't call me; I'll call you. Any questions?"

"The name," I said. "You said you had a name for us?"

"Oh, yeah, yeah." Mr. Smith rose and reached into his other pocket. He pulled out a small index card and handed it to me. It read, Felicia Nitterman and gave an address on West Twentieth Street.

"You get to know her. She can give you the goods on Miserly. You get her to trust you, she'll spill. One of yous should go after her, and the other should keep tabs on Miserly. Shadow him. Join his campaign. Join it. Get inside. That's how I want it played. Unnerstand?"

Henny and I unnerstood.

"One more time. Any questions? Get close to Nitterman; get close to Miserly."

We had no questions, and Mr. Smith departed our office, but not before pausing at the door and leaving us with a telling glance and parting words.

"Yous guys never seen me."

Henny and I sat quietly and let the last few minutes wash over us.

"You mentioned something in the bag?"

I toted up the loot—fifty C-notes—and came near fainting.

"Henny, there's five thousand bucks here."

"Holy moly." We sat in silence for another moment. Henny tossed his toothpick into the metal trashcan next to his desk and said, "I think we better collude real good on this one."

I agreed with him one hundred percent.

Four

Henny and I both knew about politics being a dirty business. Henny insisted the detective game was even dirtier, and I didn't choose to argue the point. Our brief participation in the detective game so far hadn't been particularly dirty—sneaky maybe, but I wouldn't call it dirty; that is, until Mr. Smith walked in. Henny proclaimed Mr. Smith's name to be an alias. I told him he stated the obvious. Henny said our client's name most certainly was Prudence Holiman. I shot him a look, and he explained he didn't mean the guy who walked into the office, but the client behind the guy who walked into the office. I remarked I was aware of that, too.

"Randolph Miserly is toast with us on his trail," Henny said with a smirk.

This opinion I let pass.

"One of us needs to visit this Felicia Nitterman," I said. "See what her story is."

"And one of us needs to volunteer to work in Miserly's campaign. Get on the inside, like Mr. Smith said. Hear the dirt. Get the scoop." Henny grabbed for a fresh toothpick.

"Who does which?" I asked.

"I'll take the Nitterman babe." Henny's toothpick bounced excitedly. "You join the campaign. You look more the political type."

I probably did. Henny wore his black hair combed straight back. He put something on it that made it shiny and reflect the light. I never asked what. It smelled good, though. I presented a more innocuous, blend-in-with-the-crowd appearance. Brown hair, parted on the left and combed into a slight pompadour—nothing worth a second glance. I wore a drab sport coat to work. Henny insisted on a double-breasted sport coat or suit jacket—without the pants—which he rarely buttoned. I mean he wore pants, but rarely the pants that matched the coat. And, of course, he had his toothpick and fedora.

"Done." Then, with a shrug, I said, "Might as well get started. I'll go to the bank first." I waggled the bag of Benjamins. "Then, let's go do our stuff and meet back here…when?"

"Tomorrow morning's time enough. My night in the apartment," he said. I should have mentioned earlier, maybe. Henny and I shared a very tiny, ratty studio apartment in Brooklyn, right over the Williamsburg Bridge. Each night, one of us would sleep there, get cleaned up, etc. The other would sleep in the office on a rollaway bed we kept in the office's only closet. We'd alternate. The rest room down the hall from our office satisfied any personal needs we might have for the night outside of the apartment. If we kept getting bags of Benjamins, though, we'd soon improve on this less than desirable arrangement.

"Here, don't forget her address," I asked.

Henny grabbed the index card Mr. Smith had left behind. "I'm off." Henny took a few steps toward the door and stopped. He faced me. "How great is this? It's like a Green Hornet adventure. The Hornet always fought against civic corruption." He turned and left.

I swear Henny had tears in his eyes. He referenced a 1940s' radio show he swore by. Masked crime fighter, secret identity. What a guy, Henny.

I revved up our second-hand computer and found the location of the Miserly campaign headquarters—a storefront on East Broadway in Chinatown—and off I went.

It was a gorgeous September day—blue skies, nary a cloud, a nice mix of warm in the sun; cool in the shade. At the end of a pleasant, twenty-minute walk, I opened the front door to Miserly campaign headquarters, situated between a sidewalk fruit vendor and fish store on one side and a purveyor of cheap shoes and tacky clothing on the other. The ancient building rose another five floors above the ground floor and heaven knows what went on up there.

Posters of Miserly looking his best hung on the walls. And boy, did he look good. Late middle age; abundant hair, gray in the proper spots; weathered, cable news anchor face; white shirt, red tie, and jacket visible in the from-the-shoulders-up photo. "Miserly: For the Masses" read his slogan. Aiming for the Catholic vote, I joked to myself. An older woman with long, free-flowing gray hair approached me, a welcoming smile on her face.

"How do you do?" she asked in a political-friendly tone. "Can I help you? Have you come to volunteer or are you simply lost?" She chuckled. Her standard ice-breaker, I imagined.

"No, ma'am. Not lost. I'd like to help this good man."

"Oh! That's wonderful. Please, come with me."

I followed her to a desk in the middle of the room and took a seat. She questioned me, filling out a form of some sort with my answers. Name, address, background, nothing unusual. I'd thought about my backstory during the twenty-minute walk over. I couldn't tell her I was a P. I. investigating her man, could I? I concocted a good one. A graduate student in political science at NYU, taking the semester off to work part-time accumulating the tuition for my final semester. I could see my bio impressed her.

"Oh, Mr. Lloyd, we can surely…and sorely…use you."

I'd told her my name was Alexander Lloyd so she couldn't google my real name and come up with the detective agency. I gave her the Williamsburg address as my home address. Then I played my masterstroke.

"I read the story in today's *Post*, and I'm very interested in preserving the historic residences on Mulberry Street. I live in a similar, historic type residence myself in Brooklyn." One which, truth to tell, couldn't be blown into the dustbin of history soon enough to suit me. But that's neither here nor there. I'd apparently tapped into a sweet spot on Lucinda—her name—and she gave me her standard lecture on the importance of the issue.

I agreed to address envelopes for an hour before accompanying her to a meeting of the top campaign aides. Top campaign aides! I was in…and never felt more detective-like in my life!

An hour later, Lucinda led four of us into a small space in a rear corner of the office partitioned off from the rest of the space by the corner walls and two rolling screens. Two other, older women continued with the envelopes but well out of earshot. "Here's where we are," Lucinda began. "We're seven points down in our terribly unscientific poll."

An elderly gentleman sitting next to me asked about the poll.

"Oh," Lucinda said, somewhat abashed, "we asked people going down into the subway under the Municipal Building."

The elderly gentleman nodded knowingly. "So, fifty-three, forty-six?"

"More like twenty-two, fifteen. The other sixty-three percent were mostly 'get out of my way' or colorful variations. What we desperately need is opposition research."

There seemed to be a lot of that going around, I thought.

"Holiman's having an event at six o'clock tonight, and we need someone there to hear everything she says, to take notes and report back here to Mr. Miserly."

I jumped. "To the candidate, himself?"

"Yes. At nine o'clock."

Face to face with the guy I was tracking! I volunteered.

"It makes a long day for you," Lucinda warned. "We need it, but I want to be certain you know what you're letting yourself in for."

"Mr. Miserly's election to the council is important to the neighborhood," I proclaimed, not without a certain feeling of nobility. "I'll do it!" The people at the table actually applauded my noble gesture, guilt-tripping my nobility into an incipient sense of reptility…or reptileness. Whatever. I didn't care. I had a job to do.

Lucinda gave me the details. The event would be held in a Chinatown tea parlor, which, she promised, would attract neighborhood activists to whom Holiman would spill her guts. I vowed to be present and happily accepted Lucinda's suggestion I take the rest of the afternoon off. I was already two paper cuts to the good from those lousy envelopes. I thought of joining up with Henny, but I'd neglected to commit the address of his "Nitterman babe" to memory. I called his cell but got no answer. I knew I wouldn't. He'd said more than once that neither Spade nor Marlowe ran around the city while on a case, answering a telephone ringing in his pocket. The concept was absurd, he insisted. I never or rarely, anyway, argued with Henny's predilections, so I went back to the office and started on another paperback book.

Nom Wah Tea Parlor is located on Doyers Street, a one-block, twisting 'S' of a street, branching off the lowest reach of the Bowery and snaking its way to Mott Street, the main drag of Chinatown. I made straight for a table filled with Chinese buns and pastries. Happily saddled with a plate full of free food and a Styrofoam cup of tea, I found a table off to the side, where I hoped I wouldn't be proselytized by a rabid activist. I put my notebook in front of me and took out one of the three pens I had in my jacket pocket. I would not run out of ink. I was prepared.

I picked Prudence Holiman out of the crowd in a second. Everyone took a turn at her, and she had a warm smile and a few words for everyone. She wasn't as old as I expected—still in her thirties, I guessed. And pretty good looking. She shattered my stereotype of a do-gooder—tall, lanky, homely, bespectacled, with a tightly wrapped chignon in back. Shattered it good. There were mostly Asians, both men and women, at the gathering, this being the heart of Chinatown, but a young

Caucasian woman sat down at the table next to me. She pulled a laptop out of a briefcase and flipped it open. I couldn't help but watch her prepare. She caught my stare and smiled.

"You, too?" she asked cheerfully.

"Me, too, what?"

"A reporter?"

"Oh, the notebook? In a way. How about you?"

"*World Journal.*" She seemed quite excited—perhaps carbonated is a better word. "You've never heard of it, right?"

"*World Journal*? No. Never."

"It's a Chinese newspaper. Did you know Chinatown has four newspapers?"

"No, I didn't."

"Two local ones and two editions of world-wide issues. The two local ones are covering this race very closely."

"Because of the Mulberry Street buildings?"

"No, because the council seat covers Chinatown. What do you know about the Mulberry Street buildings?"

The young lady moved her chair nearer the edge of her table and closer to me. The excitement in her voice changed to deep interest.

"I only know it's an issue."

"It is. A very important one. Do you know anything about it?"

I shook my head. "Only that Holiman is for keeping the buildings and accuses Miserly of wanting to knock them down. Miserly says she's wrong."

"Something's going on with that. I don't know what. I feel it."

"Reporter's instinct?"

"Yes! I like that!"

"Uh, may I ask you a question?"

She giggled. "You're describing my job."

I giggled back and hoped she bought it.

"You're not Chinese."

"Ooohhh. You're good."

"Do you speak Chinese?"

"No. *World Journal* has an online edition in English. Plus, if I write something really newsworthy, it gets translated and put into the paper. And I get a bit more money."

"This is how you make a living?"

She shrugged. "One bedroom apartment with three roommates. Two single beds in the living room. It's more like a dormitory. I don't need much."

Tell me about it, I thought.

"I'm Susan Denzler." She extended her hand.

"You can call me Lloyd."

"You write for…?"

"No, no. No one."

"Freelancer, eh?"

"Uh, right." I needed to change the subject but, fortunately, the subject got changed for me. Ms. Holiman began to speak, and I began to write. So did Susan Denzler. And write, type actually, she did. Every time I glanced over at her, she was pounding on the keys of her laptop. I jotted down what I could but found nothing of much note in what Prudence shared with her constituents. College activist. Paid job at Bide-a-Wee, an animal shelter. Opened a soup kitchen at the Chinatown end of the Bowery through crowd-sourcing. Paid job at a law office helping newly arrived immigrants, mostly Chinese, get their papers in order and procure whatever social assistance they were entitled to. She gracefully segued into keeping the families in the Mulberry Street buildings safe from the deprivations of greedy developers, saying it could happen in Chinatown one day. I recorded her thoughts but didn't see how any of it would help Miserly cut her down. Prudence wrapped up the meeting with a call to arms, and after the applause, the exiting began.

Susan closed her laptop and said, "You didn't take many notes."

"Enough. I have a great memory."

While Susan had been typing away, I considered the value of having access to a neighborhood news reporter. News reporters of note from big media wouldn't care too much about this particular election unless something spectacular and juicy happened. Sex scandal, bribery, embezzlement. A local reporter, though, might settle for much less. I wanted to keep in touch with Susan.

"I have another meeting at nine—in an hour or so. Care to have a drink?"

"Can't. Gotta write up my story and file it. Needs to be available for tomorrow's English and Chinese web issues. Another time?"

"Sure."

We exchanged cell numbers, and she went her way while I went mine.

I lingered over a bowl of noodles, the cheapest thing on the menu in the shop next door, and a few minutes before nine, I was back in Miserly headquarters seated at the same table as earlier with the great man himself, Lucinda, and two of the people from earlier. No one seemed to know what exactly to say or how to even begin the meeting, and the ragged, random conversation gave little indication of leading to momentous planning. Lucinda called on me to report while Miserly bent his head over his phone. "Nothing of much note," I explained. "Holiman gave her background—a world-class do-gooder—and mentioned the preservation of the Mulberry Street tenements. Don't guess any of that is much help."

Miserly pocketed his phone at the mention of Mulberry Street, and I sat at attention, hoping he'd spill the beans about his real intentions in that regard. If his public face didn't match his private intentions, we'd have him. "I don't believe her," Miserly said angrily. "She accuses me of being in cahoots with real estate, I'll accuse her of being in cahoots with real estate."

"Even if it isn't true?" Lucinda asked in a tentative tone.

"If I get elected, it won't matter what's true or what's false. She slanders me. Because I worked in real estate…because I made a ton of money in real estate…because I know everyone of note in the New York City property game…because I know David Toledo… Does that give her the right to accuse me of being in bed with real estate developers?"

Uh, yeah, I thought, it does, but I kept my opinion to myself. The eyes of everyone at the table sought shelter. Some looked up; some looked down; some looked up, down, and all around.

Miserly slammed his hand down on the table. "That's the plan, then, Lucinda. Write something up. Print up fliers. As many as we can afford. Highlight it. Holiman caters to real estate lobby."

Lucinda cleared her throat. "Do we need evidence, maybe?" she asked softly.

"Leave that to me. I'll make speeches and say the evidence will come too late—in the form of piles of old bricks on Mulberry

Street and destitute families out of the only homes they've ever known!"

The man had fire in his eyes, I'll give him that. I took a gamble.

"It's an important point to make. We need to meet her head on," I agreed, trying to spout enthusiasm. "We should meet like this in a couple days to make certain things stay on track."

Miserly pointed at me. "Good idea. Your name again?"

I gave it.

"Good man. Forty-eight hours. Wednesday. Nine o'clock. Right here." He banged the table again.

I happily noted it would be my night to sleep in the office, so I'd have no need to schlep back to Brooklyn and the grimy apartment.

"Anything I can do for you tomorrow, Mr. Miserly?" I asked.

"You're free?"

"Yes, sir."

"Give me your number. I may want you."

We parted and I walked back to the Centre Street office. Henny wasn't there, of course, so I'd have to wait until tomorrow morning for a report. I performed my evening toilet in the elegant confines of the third floor men's room and rolled out the bed. I read a couple of chapters before calling it a day.

Five

I was at my desk when Henny walked in next morning, sans toothpick but sporting a black fedora with a red feather. His dark blue, double-breasted jacket flapped open.

"How'd you do?" was my first question.

He held up one finger as he tossed his fedora at a coat rack in the corner. He walked over, picked his hat up from the floor, and hung it gently on a protruding hook of decorative metal.

"You first," he said, glaring at the offending coat rack.

I filled Henny in on my day.

When I finished, Henny said, "Mr. Smith should be pleased you've gotten inside so fast." Lines formed between Henny's eyes. "He hasn't been here yet, has he?"

"No. So, come on. Did you find the Nitterman woman yesterday?"

"Yes and no."

I tilted my head and frowned. "You want to explain?"

"The address on the index card was in Chelsea, remember? West Twentieth Street, the four-hundred block. All nice brownstones. Not too different looking from Gilly's block. I found the exact address and checked the mailboxes in the vestibule. Four mailboxes. Four apartments. The third floor mailbox read: Felicia Nitterman. There was no doorman to grill or pay off, of course. All I could do was case the joint all day. About two o'clock, a young woman comes out…"

"Nitterman?"

"No, I don't think so. I could see she came out of the ground floor apartment. Besides, she had a baby carriage and another little kid holding on to it. Off they went. Five o'clock, this guy walks up, stands out front, and makes a phone call. A minute later, another guy comes out the front door. The two of them hold hands and go wandering down the sidewalk. For sure, no Felicia Nitterman there. Around six, a young woman, had to be in her twenties, enters the building, but I couldn't see what floor she went to. Didn't matter. Half an hour, she comes out wearing a different dress, fancier, and walks the half block east to Ninth Avenue. Destination: Bocca di Bacco, on the corner."

"A restaurant?"

"Yeah. I figure this might be Nitterman, so I follow her. She sits at the bar. I sit at the bar, but I leave a chair between us respectfully empty. She keeps checking her phone. I figure she's meeting somebody, so I better act quick. I lean over and say: I'm sorry. Don't I know you from somewhere? Boy, does she give me a look! No, seriously, I say. Aren't you Felicia Nitterman? I could see she relaxes a little.

"'No, she's my neighbor. How'd you get us confused?'

"You two must resemble one another.

"'Not really. She's at least ten years older than I am. She's rarely around, though. I hardly ever see her.'

"Turns out she didn't know where Nitterman works, or what she did, or anything about her. Knew the name from the mailbox and from passing her on the stairs a couple times. Said she wasn't very friendly. Chatty was the word she used, not friendly. Saw her once going upstairs ahead of her with a man."

"She get a look at the man?"

"Only the back."

I shrugged and spread my hands.

"What? We talked, then the guy she was waiting for showed up, and they moved to a table."

"You go back to the building?"

"Not right away. I had to eat something. I could only afford one appetizer—a great mushroom bruschetta—and a beer. Two things—twenty bucks with the tip! About three days' grocery money. Anyway, I went back to the building after I ate, but the third floor windows stayed dark. I'm going back today. I wanted to come in and report to you, so you could fill in Mr. Smith if he showed up. And to check my mail."

"Henny, we never get any mail."

"Not yet, but you never know."

Henny retrieved his hat from the rack and left.

My phone rang—Miserly asking me to join him for a lunchtime meeting at the Pastorino Domino and Social Club on Mulberry Street.

"Is the meeting open to the public?" I asked.

"Sure. I'm looking for votes, not privacy."

We hung up and I called Susan, my new favorite reporter, clued her in, and promised to see her there.

I saw Susan coming along the sidewalk from the opposite direction as I strolled along Mulberry Street. We arrived in front of the Pastorino Domino and Social Club at exactly the same moment. I considered this a good sign. Not so much for the case, but for the incipient crush I was developing on the young lady.

"Hi," she said brightly. "Shall we go in?"

We found two seats on wooden, folding chairs in the rear of the large room. A small, scratched up bar lined one wall. An opening in the rear wall showed a small kitchen beyond. A podium with a skinny mike attached stood center stage, if you will, and chairs, which were filling up quickly, ranged across the floor.

"Did you read my piece?" Susan asked, eyes aglow.

"Great work," I said. I hadn't read it.

"You didn't read it," she said joshingly.

"I don't read Chinese."

She frowned. "It was posted in English. I told you. Read it. *World Journal* dot com."

"I will. I will. Been busy."

"Doing what?"

"Busy in the campaign."

Another frown. "I thought you were a reporter. You're not, are you?"

"Well, no. Not really. In a way, kind of." Miserly walked in, and the conversation got postponed. Thank goodness. When Miserly beckoned me, I noted the puzzled look on Susan's face. I got out of my chair, and Miserly led me into a corner.

"You're doing great work," Miserly complimented.

I wondered what work he meant. Great envelope licking? I let him talk.

"I want you to continue your opposition research on Holiman. Your work's been terrific."

I couldn't imagine what good work I'd done, but I decided to take advantage.

"I'll report back to you again? Wednesday night still?"

"I'm gonna make a big push over the weekend. Stay with Holiman all week. Where she goes, you go. Don't leave her. Skip tomorrow night's meeting. There'll be another meeting Friday night at my headquarters. I'll need everything you have. Seven o'clock. Be on time. I have a speech to make nearby at nine."

"Okay. Got it."

"What's that all about?" Susan asked when I sat down again.

"I'm undercover," I said out of the side of my mouth.

"You're undercover?" she repeated dismissively. "We'll talk when we're done here. I may have to do a story on you."

When I faced her, she was facing at me. I looked back at the podium where Miserly had launched into his speech. Two minutes in, he waved a stack of papers he said were petitions from residents of the Mulberry Street buildings and buildings nearby supporting him. The neighborhood was paramount, he said. Elect him, he argued, to preserve what was right.

He got his applause, and things broke up.

"Lunch on me," Susan said. Not asked… said. What could I do but accept the offer?

Susan led me to the corner of Broome and Mulberry Streets, a place called Grotto Azzurra, a place I never would have gone on my own, considering my financial situation.

"Aren't you on duty?" I asked when Susan ordered a white wine.

"It's lunch hour. Have a drink."

I ordered a glass of red wine. We chatted, we ordered, and her interrogation began. I didn't stand up well against it, and before five minutes passed, I'd told her I'd been hired to "look into the election," and my job was tailing Prudence Holiman. Susan knew about protecting sources, so she didn't even ask who hired me, though I presumed she thought me in the employ of Randolph Miserly. If she did, she had it backwards.

"Hired to investigate Prudence Holiman," Susan stated, merely thinking aloud, not questioning me. I didn't contradict her thought.

She went on. "I wish there were something crooked about this election. I've applied for jobs at the *Times*, the *Post*, and the *Daily News*." Her eyes looked a challenge into mine, as if she expected me to laugh at her ambition.

"A worthy profession. Bernstein, Woodward."

"Yes! Exactly! That's what I need. A story of corruption that makes it into the real newspapers, not simply the *World Journal*. We need more Richard Nixons."

It was the first time I'd ever heard anyone say that.

"Keep plugging," I encouraged. "There's plenty of evil in the world. You'll find your Nixon."

She giggled, and my heart swooned.

She said, "If you come across something in your investigation, please give it to me and no one else. Especially not the big three newspapers."

"You will be my outlet, I promise." Our lunches arrived, and the biographical portions of the conversation turned banal.

When Susan reached for the bill, I felt bad but quickly got over it.

I asked, "Can I see you again? I mean like this?"

Her expression showed she expected more. I wasn't stupid. I got the point.

"How about dinner on me?" I went on. "Friday?" I leaned over the table. "I'm reporting back to Miserly headquarters at seven Friday night. I have an ear in each camp. Maybe I'll have uncovered something by then. Dinner at eight?"

We set a meeting place, Golden Unicorn, a Chinese restaurant on East Broadway, and went our separate ways.

I spent the rest of the week following Prudence Holiman around. Nothing happened. She made speeches, always including the Mulberry Street issue of preserving the old housing; rallied the half-dozen volunteers who showed up in her headquarters each day; and made two radio appearances—one on WCBS and one on WINS.

Henny had an equally unspectacular few days. He stood outside of Felicia Nitterman's brownstone until, he said, he felt like he'd taken root. His random strolls up and down the block had given him a nodding acquaintance with the family with the two children, the two gentlemen who went for walks together, as well as the woman he'd chatted up in Bocca di Bacco, but no Felicia Nitterman.

Friday rolled around. Before setting out for the day, Henny and I discussed the very real likelihood we'd have nothing to report to Mr. Smith. Neither one of us wanted to say what was on our minds regarding that possibility, other than we'd better find something to report. Then, out of the blue, Mr. Smith arrived. He didn't knock a rat-a-tat friendly request for entry. Rather, three dull thuds sounded on the door, same as on his first visit, and we knew who stood on our threshold.

Henny got the door and in came Mr. Smith, who went right to the client chair and sat.

"Good morning, gentlemen. You got any news for me?"

I looked at Henny; Henny looked at me.

"Well? How 'bout you?" Mr. Smith indicated Henny.

Henny gulped in preparation. "I've been outside Felicia Nitterman's building every day."

"You ain't there now."

"Lloyd and I check in here in the morning to compare notes."

"What notes? I don't see no notes. You ain't got no notes."

"Uh, well we don't know we ain't got no notes until we…we…know we ain't got no notes."

The left corner of Mr. Smith's lip rose, and he shook an index finger my way and then Henny's way.

"You stay on Felicia Nitterman. All night you gotta. Hear?"

Mr. Smith glared at me, but I pointed to Henny.

"Nitterman's his," I said.

"You hear?" Smith growled in Henny's direction.

"I hear."

"I'll be back."

When the office door closed, I said, "Guess we better get back to work."

Henny shoved a toothpick in his mouth, went for his hat, and as he was leaving, he grumbled, "'Nitterman's his.'"

"Well, she is. I couldn't…" Henny slammed the door behind him.

I checked Prudence Holiman's schedule on her campaign's website and set out. Oh, the drudgery. I sat through another four excruciating speeches, and if that weren't bad enough, she said the same thing everywhere she went, practically word for word. I've read about staying on message and how it was an honorable thing for a politician to do, but Prudence's hewing to her one narrow roadway had me considering taking the weekend off and spending it in any lunatic asylum offering free meals and Netflix. I couldn't follow her directly after her speeches concluded because she left wherever she'd spoken in a big, black car. I could only scurry to the next place on the list, either by subway or, more often, by walking as fast as I could to keep up.

After a long, dreary day, I made my way to Miserly's headquarters for the seven o'clock meeting, wondering how the hell what I was doing would provide any pertinent information for Mr. Smith. I presumed Henny would let me know the moment he came across anything and made a second presumption Henny wouldn't hold a grudge from this morning.

The usual bunch of us, led by Lucinda, sat at the table in headquarters, and before asking us to report, Miserly offered some good news.

"We're within five points of Holiman," he spouted.

I wondered whether that meant twenty percent to fifteen percent with sixty-five percent not giving a rat's ass. Excuse my language, but my mood had deteriorated considerably during this lousiest, most tedious of days.

"We need one big item to take her down. Anybody?"

Nobody.

"You, Mr. Lloyd?"

"No, she gives the same speech everywhere. She highlights her support of the Mulberry Street neighborhood as proof of her commitment to the little man." I shrugged. Mr. Smith's image floated across my consciousness. I had to get something on Miserly, not Holiman. It was a health issue. My health.

"How about you?" I asked. "You have any hints or clues about something we could bring her down on?" I felt it a bold question, and when the others at the table turned my way, I knew it was a bold question.

"No," Miserly said peevishly. "That's why I have you people doing opposition research. Stay on her."

"If I may," I said before Miserly could adjourn the meeting. "She's hitting Mulberry Street hard. Make certain you do the same. The election may turn on Mulberry Street. Your plans for Mulberry Street are the same as hers, aren't they?" I held my breath.

"Of course they are, no matter what she says," Miserly answered irritably, and we broke up.

Damn, I thought. There didn't seem to be anything to catch the man on. I didn't want anyone from headquarters to see me meet Susan, so I took a long walk around the block and came down to Golden Unicorn from the opposite direction. Susan already had a table for us and had even ordered. Vegetable fried rice and spicy bean curd without the ground pork. A vegetarian, I learned. Good for my wallet; bad for my stomach. I'd get a hamburger later.

We exchanged our news of the day.

"You find your Watergate story?" I asked good-naturedly.

"Are you making fun of me?"

"No, not at all." Well, maybe a little. "What'd you do today?"

"I spent the day, a wasted day, looking into Prudence Holiman's background. You know she worked in an animal shelter, then started a soup kitchen? A soup kitchen! Freakin' Mother Teresa."

"She brings it up in every speech." I told Susan about my tedious day. "I really wish I could help you." Then my phone rang. I gave it a look. Henny! "I have to take this."

Henny babbled at me ninety miles an hour.

"On my way," I said and slid the phone back into my pocket. "You're coming with me, Susan. We might have something for you."

"We? Who we? Go where? We haven't finished our food."

"Eat quick and I'll fill you in."

Henny had found Felicia Nitterman. A woman he'd not seen before entered the building he'd come to know so well. A moment later, the lights in the third floor apartment came on. Henny's instincts rose; so said Henny. Half an hour later, the third floor lights went out, and a moment afterwards the woman leaves the building. Henny followed her to the same neighborhood restaurant the previous woman had visited. She took a back, corner table; Henny grabbed a bar chair and watched her in the mirror backing the bar. Henny made a point of how cleverly he watched her in the mirror. A big, black car pulled up outside. A man got out, entered the restaurant, and joined Nitterman at her table. They were there now, and Susan and I were on the way.

In the cab Susan peppered me with questions. All I could tell her was Henny and I were a team acting on a tip. I said I'd tell her more about Henny later, and the tip was confidential.

"Compose yourself and don't stare," I advised Susan when we exited the taxi.

"Don't tell me how to act. Compose your own self."

"I'm composed." I took her arm, and she glared at me. "It'll look better if we're a couple. Casual. Normal." She didn't argue or pull away. We sashayed into the restaurant and joined Henny at the bar. Henny, Susan, and I played it cool. I made the appropriate introductions. "Where are they?" I said softly.

"Table in the back corner. No, don't turn. Slide over. There, in the mirror."

Susan and I studied the reflection.

"You sure that's Felicia Nitterman?" I asked, looking at Susan.

"That's her. Felicia Nitterman. Absolutely."

"No it's not," Susan said. She turned and looked at the real thing for a moment. She spun back on her stool and said, "That is Prudence Holiman. And do you see who's with her?"

I took a look at the real thing. "I see. Who is it?"

"You're kidding, right?"

"No. Henny, you know him?"

Henny chanced a non-reflective examination of the couple. He shrugged.

"Prudence Holiman is having dinner with David Toledo, the biggest real estate developer in all of New York City."

"Mulberry Street!" I said.

"Mulberry Street," Susan repeated.

"Watergate," I said.

Susan smiled.

Six

Henny and I sat in place as Susan took a discreet photo of the couple with her phone, got up, and walked over to Prudence Holiman's table.

Henny leaned over and said, "This is so much better than any Green Hornet adventure I ever listened to."

"Maybe we should become radio heroes instead of real-life heroes," I replied.

We watched. There were polite smiles all around to begin. Suddenly, an anxious look exploded onto the right profile of Prudence's face, which was all Henny and I could see of it. David Toledo's left profile congealed into a frown. He waggled his finger at Susan, who merely nodded her head twice, looked directly at Prudence, and said something. Henny and I could hear Prudence's abbreviated yelp even at a distance. Toledo pushed his chair back and said something to Susan, who returned him a grim smile and waggled her own finger back and forth at him slowly. Toledo rose and stormed from the restaurant. Henny and I averted our eyes until he passed by. Susan made a friendly gesture toward Prudence, obviously asking whether she could sit. Prudence jutted out her jaw defiantly for a moment, then bowed her head. Susan took a chair. Prudence took a handkerchief from her handbag and dabbed at her eyes. Susan reached across the table and put her hand on top of Prudence's, then leaned in and said something. Prudence nodded, both women rose, and together they walked slowly from the restaurant. Susan glanced at me slyly, her eyes briefly making big circles.

"I think," I said, "we're going to make Mr. Smith unhappy."

"Unhappy… Oh. We were supposed to get dirt on Miserly, weren't we?"

"We were."

"We didn't, did we?"

"No, we didn't."

"Want some mushroom bruschetta? Fills you up."

"Did Sam Spade or Philip Marlowe ever eat mushroom bruschetta?"

"I don't think so. But we're not Sam Spade and Philip Marlowe."

"You can say that again."

I stayed on the office rollaway that night, hoping Susan might give me a desperate call for help. She didn't. My cell rang but not until two o'clock in the morning.

"I hope you're awake," came Susan's bubbling voice.

"I answered the phone, didn't I?" my groggy, slurred voice responded.

"It's up."

"The jig? The moon? The stock market?"

"No, silly. My story."

"I didn't know you had a story."

"Hmm. You must have gotten up on the wrong side of the bed."

"I didn't get up on any side of the bed. I'm in bed."

"My story's up; it's posted, and no one has it but me—of Prudence Holiman posing as Felicia Nitterman and having a Twentieth Street love nest, paid for by David Toledo, who planned to have her use her influence to knock down the Mulberry Street houses for a development he wanted to build. She took me down the street to her apartment and told me everything. Her candidacy is in the dumpster. She's leaving the race. Miserly will be your new city councilman."

Susan's report had awakened me plenty. Mr. Smith and his looming unhappiness kept me awake until morning. Susan invited me to dinner the next night to celebrate. Celebrate Henny's and my demise, I thought.

I booted up our computer and read her story. To condense: Prudence Holiman met David Toledo when Toledo's wife got a rescue dog from the animal shelter where Prudence worked. Toledo came in with his wife. The wife left with a puppy; Toledo left with a mistress. Toledo financed her soup kitchen, thus earning her everlasting affection. He got her the Chelsea apartment for their private use, thus earning her even more everlasting affection. When Toledo found a way to surreptitiously finance her campaign for city council in exchange for the necessary shenanigans to raze the buildings on Mulberry

Street, Prudence jumped at the offer as a demonstrable, concrete way to return her great affection for the many favors Toledo had showered on her. Or so Susan quoted her. The story ended with a gut-wrenching account of Prudence's remorse for being a two-faced hussy—my words, not Susan's—and her pledge to drop out of the race immediately.

The next day's headline in the *Daily News* read: WHO IS FELICIA NITTERMAN? The headline in the *Post* read: CITY COUNCIL CANDIDATE IN BED WITH REAL ESTATE MAGNATE. The *Times* ran the story on page one, beneath the fold. The *Post* and *Daily News* both used the photo Susan had taken with her phone, and Susan was right. Her reporting had consigned Prudence Holiman to the dustbin of history; Miserly had a city council seat waiting.

Susan and I had a nice dinner on Saturday. She thanked me for bringing her in on such a dynamite story. I explained everything about Henny and me, except for the part about Mr. Smith. I knew enough not to go there. It was my night in the apartment, and that's where Susan and I ended up as her gratitude continued to flow. Enough said about that.

After a quiet, somber Sunday, Henny and I waited for the ax to fall, presuming Mr. Smith to be an ax murderer. Monday, nothing. Tuesday, Miserly's uncontested election win. Wednesday, at two o'clock in the afternoon, three familiar thuds sounded on our office door. When Henny reached for a toothpick, he spilled the whole box onto the floor. I jumped up, nearly pulling a muscle in my calf. I opened the door, and in walked Mr. Smith, his right hand buried deep in his jacket pocket.

"Hello, M…Mr. Smith," I stuttered. I hurried back to my chair, hoping not to get plugged in the back.

Mr. Smith's head went slowly on a swivel from Henny to me to Henny to me. Wondering which one of us to obliterate first, I imagined. Then something I'd never seen before happened. Mr. Smith smiled.

"Yous guys did one hell of a job. You couldn'ta done better if you'da knowed what you was doing. Pulling in that reporter dame was genius, pure genius."

Henny had slouched down in his chair under Mr. Smith's gaze but now straightened.

"You said you wanted the best detectives in town on the job," he said.

Again Mr. Smith's head went on a slow swivel, his smile gone.

"Yous guys are probably wondering why I'm so happy. I sent you after Miserly, and you took down Holiman."

"That has crossed my mind," I said, still not sure Mr. Smith wasn't doing a little cat and mouse with us.

"I'll tell ya what I can. I got a client. His mother and ninety-two-year-old grandmother, a wonderful woman, live in one of them apartments that was gonna be torn down by Holiman and Toledo. My client, he didn't want that. He likes things the way they are. We knew about the little parties Holiman and Toledo had in their lovey-dovey apartment. That's why I sent you there."

"That explains Henny, but you sent me to spy on Miserly," I pointed out.

"The…uh, persons at Miserly's place who told you to follow Holiman around for…" Mr. Smith chuckled. "…opposition research are friends of ours. You went where I sent you; they sent you where I told 'em to."

"Lucinda and Miserly? You told both of them?"

Mr. Smith's eyebrows lifted slowly, and he leaned his head back a little. "Yeah, Alexander." Mr. Smith smiled knowingly. "So?"

"Sheesh. You have friends everywhere."

"You could say that."

Henny had a question. "If you knew about the two of them, why didn't you go to the newspapers yourself? Why depend on us? Suppose we failed."

"If you failed, there were other…more dramatic ways we coulda…heh, heh, heh…affected the outcome of this election. But quieter is better. We didn't want no fingerprints on anything. You know what I mean? And in case you don't remember—lemme remind you. Yous guys never seen me. I was never here. You don't know me. None of this ever happened. Nothing comes back my way. See? No fingerprints. Capeesh?"

Henny and I capeeshed in a very copacetic manner.

Mr. Smith kept his hand in his jacket pocket the whole time, and then, when he pulled his hand out of his pocket, both Henny and I sat up straight, very attentive. Henny made a funny noise.

"What, yous two nervous? Relax."

Mr. Smith withdrew a white envelope from his pocket. "Who's the treasurer?"

I couldn't get my mouth to work so I raised my hand. Mr. Smith tossed the envelope onto my desk.

"A bonus from my employer cause yous done so good."

"Employer? I thought you had a client, not an employer."

"Let's say…he's the boss."

"The boss?" I crackled.

"Yeah, the boss. You can call him…Don, you wanna." Mr. Smith let out a hearty laugh. "This bonus is to insure no fingerprints. And, uh, you know there's another different, sure way to avoid fingerprints what don't involve no bonus, don't you?"

"What's that?" Henny asked.

"Cut off the hands and toss them into the river. No hands; no fingerprints." Mr. Smith smiled.

"Cut off…?" I sputtered.

"My hands can't swim," Henny remarked.

"So take the bonus, then. It's easier. I'll be seeing yous." Mr. Smith headed to the door. He paused and burst into laughter again. "Your hands can't swim. That's funny. Your partner's a funny guy. I gotta tell Freddy the Finger that one."

Mr. Smith opened the door and left. The last thing we heard was laughter, along Mr. Smith muttering, "His hands can't swim."

After a moment of quiet contemplation, Henny said, "We really do good when we don't know what the hell we're doing. Two cases in a row. What's in the envelope?"

I counted. "Three thousand more."

"That's ten thousand bucks we made so far. We got enough, you think, to get that empty studio apartment on the sixth floor in our building?"

"I guess."

"Let's take the rest of the day off and do that."

"Think we should?"

Henny opened the bottom drawer of his desk and lifted out the Boone's That's All.

"First, let's celebrate. I'll spring for some paper cups later today."

"Paper cups? Get some glasses, for Pete's sake."

"Spade drank from paper cups in his office."

I couldn't argue against such canonical evidence.

Henny rolled up a piece of printer paper for each of us and poured.

"To continued success," I said.

We drank. Then we drank again.

Seven

The Missing Emerald

The week finished on a quiet note. Susan reapplied to the *Times*, the *Post* and the *Daily News*, her scoop on the city council election giving her fifteen minutes of notoriety she intended to cash in on. She promised to let me know the results. On Saturday afternoon, she stopped over my new sixth-floor studio apartment, furniture-less, other than a mattress, and equally as ratty as the apartment Henny'd kept—he and I flipped a coin to see who moved up three floors. Believe me, there was no heartbreak in my allowing him to keep the furniture.

Susan helped me test out the newly delivered mattress but couldn't stay for more than one test. She had a date that night. I didn't try to make sense of her behavior; I simply went with the flow. We would continue to see one another, she vowed, and her promise was good enough for me. Gift horse in the mouth and such.

The following week dragged by with little to do. More accurately, with nothing to do. Henny did go out and buy a five-dollar fedora at a street stand in Chinatown and spent the week trying to throw it onto the hat rack talon. He managed a 99.9% failure rate but hooted like an owl when he made a shot. The boy was driving me crazy. I hoped something would come along soon. I sat dreaming of Susan. But then…

"Yip yip."

Henny straightened from picking his hat up off the floor, where he'd tossed it for what seemed to me the ten thousandth time. "You hear that?" he asked.

"Yip yip."

"I hear it." The sound came from outside our office door—a high pitched, snapped off yelp, followed by a knock on the door, and another "yip yip."

Henny hung up his hat, grabbed a toothpick, buttoned his double-breasted, brown pin-striped jacket, and went to greet our visitor. In walked an older woman, buxom and large. A tiny, well-coiffured, white dog pranced ahead of her at the end of a red leash studded with…diamonds? The dog looked around and gave another "yip yip," and that will be the last "yip yip" I record unless it becomes absolutely necessary. The woman wore a midnight blue dress studded with…diamonds? A tiny, circular, blue hat crowned her head of short, brown, curly hair. Whatever she and the dog were studded with sparkled in the sunlight streaming through our two office windows. The dog leaped into our client chair.

"Down, Puffy."

The dog looked askance at his or her mistress.

"Please, Puffy! Down!"

The dog reluctantly settled for a spot on the floor.

"Please be seated," I said, and the diamond-studded lady replaced diamond-studded Puffy in our client chair.

"Puffy, shh. I believe you are Mr. Henny and Mr. Lloyd?"

We weren't Mister Henny and Mister Lloyd, but we were Henny and Lloyd, and that would suffice. If it took being labelled Misters to get hired, we were in.

"Yes," I said.

"Mrs. Giles Raymond referred me to you. I believe you did some work for her."

So Margarita snared old Gilly after all.

"We did some fine work for the former Ms. Daniels," Henny offered.

"Mr. Raymond is my financial adviser, and I trust him implicitly. His wife recommended you. I am here."

She sat, her head tilted slightly back, as if she'd explained everything, which she hadn't. I interrupted the awkward silence.

"Well, uh, we welcome you. May…may we know your name?"

"I…" She paused dramatically. "…am Arabella von Schneiderhoven." She bobbed her head definitively.

Henny rose and made a slight bow. I thought, for a moment, he would click his heels.

"Welcome, Ms. von Schneiderhaffen," he said.

"Hoven," she corrected.

"Hoven?" said Henny.

"Hoven, not haffen."

"Ah, yes. Welcome, Ms. Schleiderhoven."

"Schneider, not Schleider! Arabella von Schneiderhoven!" the woman repeated with cutting precision and a marked increase in decibels. "And it's missus, not miz!"

Henny muttered a decrepit third welcome, omitting all nomenclature, and sat down.

"How can we help you?" I asked.

The woman gave Henny a frigid look before addressing herself to me.

"I am giving a party this weekend, tomorrow night to be exact. I would like you to be there. Both of you." She glared at Henny. "I think."

"Oh, yes," I put in quickly. "We work best together—a team. I'm sure Ms….Mrs. Raymond would vouch for that."

"Well." Mrs. von Schneiderhoven gave herself a little shakeup.

"What would we do at your party?" I asked.

"My daughter has gotten engaged. Finally. We have a tradition in the von Schneiderhoven family. An emerald, a beautiful, Columbian emerald."

A rapturous glow suffused the face of Arabella von Schneiderhoven. When Arabella (I'll call her Arabella. Typing von Schneiderhoven repeatedly, without error, is beyond human capability) returned from the dream world, where the beautiful Columbian emerald had taken her, she continued.

"The emerald is set in a gold ring on a bed of diamonds."

"I'll bet it's nice," Henny said.

Arabella sniffed in disdain. "Nice," she mumbled. "Yes, it's nice," she added cattily. "Its monetary value is incalculable. Its value to my family even more so."

I wondered what more than incalculable toted up to.

"It has been passed daughter to daughter for a very long time, and tomorrow evening, I pass it on to Ariadne."

"Ariadne's your daughter?" Henny asked.

Arabella sent another icy glare Henny's way.

"No, Ariadne is the wife of the trash man. Didn't I just say the emerald passed daughter to daughter?"

Henny nodded and sat back.

Again, I jumped in to keep things on track.

"What would you like us to do?"

"You will protect the emerald. I'm having a number of people over to celebrate the beginnings of this new union. I will bring out the emerald at the proper time. You will stand near it, protect it." She bobbed her head again. "It will look good. The emerald deserves a decent show."

"You expect someone to snatch it?" Henny asked.

A growl issued from Arabella's throat. When Arabella growled, Puffy growled.

Another jump-in from me.

"I'm sure no one in Mrs. von Schneiderhoven's circle could possibly be suspected of such a thing."

Arabella gave me a polite smile and another head bob.

"Exactly," she said. "I am merely providing the gravitas such a moment requires." Her smile waned. "But, of course, you are there to be certain the emerald is secure. Now, I will provide bedrooms for you and…him…tomorrow evening in my house. Have I told you I live on Long Island?"

"You have not," I said.

I took Arabella's information, and she gave us instructions on when we'd be picked up by her driver next afternoon and what to bring and how to dress. An embarrassing moment arrived.

"I have to tell you, Mrs. von Schneiderhoven, neither Mr. Henny nor I has a tuxedo."

"I thought as much." She handed me a card. "I've informed Alphonse you'd be in this afternoon. He will have something suitable for you."

The card read simply, THE SARTORIAL SALON OF ALPHONSE. The address was Fifty-Sixth Street and Fifth Avenue. I couldn't wait to meet Alphonse.

"He will not close until you arrive. Do you have any questions?"

I did. Our fee, but how to phrase it. Arabella, though, behaved admirably and helped me out.

"No questions? Good. As to your fee. I will have Giles send you a check on Monday." She rose without mentioning an amount, but I felt pretty sure we could trust the old gal.

"Remember, a car will be downstairs tomorrow afternoon at three. Good day. Come, Puffy."

Puffy got to his feet and, in a show of defiance, jumped onto the client chair and glared at Henny. He or she gave a final "yip yip" before following his or her mistress from the premises.

"The old lady doesn't like me, but she ain't no Mary Astor," Henny sniped. "She ain't no Nora Charles. And that mangy dog ain't no Asta."

"If she were Nora Charles, she could solve her own problems. She wouldn't need us," I pointed out.

"She doesn't have any problems, yet."

"Wait'll we get there," I mumbled.

Henny frowned, and we headed out to see Alphonse.

While we rode the subway uptown, I had a thought. Arabella seemed to be a regular customer of Alphonse. If so, Alphonse could possibly give Henny and me a little insight into the family. I didn't entirely buy her story about simply putting on a show. If Arabella hired two detectives to watch over the emerald, she must think the emerald needed watching over. Henny agreed.

Alphonse rushed from the back of his establishment—I cannot bring myself to call it a store. It was well above being a store. And calling it a salon sounded a bit too poofy for my taste—when the salesperson told him we'd arrived. He was a slight man with a few strands of hair on the crown of his head and a ring of Friar Tuck hair encircling it. He spoke with a French accent, which you may use your imagination to duplicate. He also had a thin mustache which was the widest mustache I'd ever seen. While not exactly ear to ear, it almost made the coast-to-coast journey. Only the lack of a beret prevented his being a prototype.

"Ah, yes," he gushed. "*Monsieur* Henry and *Monsieur* Floyd."

Henny and I shared a glance at one another and nodded our heads simultaneously. It wasn't worth the bother. We'd be whoever he wanted us to be.

"Gabriel, Gabriel," Alphonse called, slapping his hands together three times. He accented Gabriel on the last syllable, by the way. "Gabriel will measure. We have some ready-made tuxedos perfect for you. Mrs. von Schneiderhoven has specified only the finest. Measure, Gabriel, measure."

Henny and I stretched, turned, and spread while Gabriel, pins sticking out of his mouth and tape measure draped over shoulders, went to work.

"Mr. Alphonse," I began, "you seem to be quite friendly with the von Schneiderhovens."

"Yes, yes, yes. But, of course. I have dressed her husband for decades. He is so much older than she is, you know. Eighty, at least. Measure the arm again, Gabriel. The arm."

"Have you met the daughter who's getting engaged?"

"Ariadne, oh my."

Alphonse put his fingers to his lips and pointed to Gabriel.

"Quick, quick, Gabriel. Finish up and find two suitable ensembles for the gentlemen." Gabriel worked his magic with his tape measure and scurried into the back of the establishment.

"You were mentioning Ariadne," I prodded. Alphonse seemed to be quite the gossip.

"Mrs. von Schneiderhoven is ecstatic over Ariadne's finding a mate."

He made it sound like Arabella had finally located a randy male panda and introduced it into the female's cage at the zoo.

"She is newly turned thirty, and Mrs. von Schneiderhoven has been so worried. She has cried to me. Right back there. Tears, real tears. So worried Ariadne would go unmarried."

Henny offered his thoughts.

"Is this Ariadne a looker? Is she pretty? What's the problem?"

Alphonse bowed his head, threw up his arms defensively, and did a few embarrassed dance steps.

"All I can say is, the Mrs. was worried. But she is happy now!" Alphonse concluded gleefully.

Gabriel returned lugging two large, thin cardboard boxes. He handed one to Henny, the other to me.

"The feet, Gabriel. Have you measured the feet? They must wear shoes. *Sacre bleu*! You send them away without shoes? Measure the feet!"

Poor Gabriel tossed his arms into the air and fled to the rear. He came back instantly with one of those sliding gadgets shoe people use to size your feet. We sat; Gabriel measured; he gave us two shoeboxes; we thanked Alphonse and left.

"New shoes, too!" Henny gushed when we were out of range. "I'm starting to like the old biddy a lot more."

"We're running with the big dogs, Henny," I agreed.

"Speaking of dogs—what do you think this Ariadne looks like? Alphonse nearly had a stroke when I asked."

"Why should we care? We don't have to marry her."

Henny laughed. I laughed. We returned to Williamsburg and our separate apartments to await the dawning of the new day.

Eight

Henny and I felt odd next morning taking the subway to our office in our tuxes, but we felt right at home in the rear of the gigantic, chauffeured black Lincoln Arabella provided. I thanked my lucky stars Henny'd left his hat with the red feather and his toothpicks home. Despite his assurances and protests, though, I did pat him down before we left. The traffic was dreadful, but what cared we? The driver asked what kind of music we'd like to listen to, and Henny, naturally, suggested Glenn Miller. It would put us "In the Mood," he joked. The driver did whatever he needed to do, and Glenn Miller joined us for the long, two-hour ride.

Arabella's Long Island estate was a pip! A lengthy driveway bordered by tall trees beginning to show some color led to the house, mansion, manor—Henny insisted on calling it a manor—which looked like the Alamo with its wide, strong, stone walls and fancy-Christmas-ball design, sort of like a bulbous pagoda, above the front door. The driver silenced Glenn Miller, and we exited the car. As if by magic, the front door of the manor house opened, and in we strolled. A young lady in a short, black dress wearing a white apron and what looked like a nurse's cap led us across a wide, marble-floored entry and into a room large enough to be called a ballroom. We saw Arabella, dressed in a long white gown and crowned with a tiara, bustling about, ordering this to go here and that to go there. A very impressive chandelier hung from the ceiling, mid-room.

"Oh, you've arrived," she said when she saw Henny and me. "Look things over. The party will be held in this room. People should be arriving anytime now." Off she went to direct the placement of some newly delivered flowers. Henny and I sauntered about, circling a long table set for thirty-six, which bisected the room, stretching from near the entry door to near the wall of windows opposite, which overlooked the grounds. Name cards sat atop each dinner plate. We circumnavigated the table without seeing our names on any of the cards.

"We eat in the kitchen with the help, I guess," Henny groused.

Many chairs, both cushioned and not, spread around the room. An array of liquor covered a table next to a bar placed in front of the windows to the left of the dining table, where a white-shirted, black bow-tied bartender fussed with his glasses and slices of lemons and limes; bowls of olives and bright red cherries; and napkins and little red plastic stirrers. I noted a vat of ice cubes nestled under the bar. I couldn't remember ever having seen such a colorful array of booze. Clear bottles of vodka and gin. Multiple shades of brown for different Scotches, bourbons, whiskeys, brandy, and Cognac. Yellow Galliano, green crème de menthe, Red Alize Passion Liqueur—I couldn't wait to see who drank that—Dekuyper Blue Curacao. With the sun shining into the room onto the array of booze, the liquor table looked like a Christmas tree lying on its side, its lights lit and twinkling.

After we'd seen everything there was to see, Henny and I returned to a busy, busy Arabella.

"Our first guests have arrived," she said. "Stay alert."

"Where's the rock?" Henny asked.

Arabella winced.

"The rock?" she repeated with slow, pained enunciation.

"We can't protect the rock unless we know where it is," Henny explained. His argument sounded reasonable to me.

"The emerald is in the safe and will be brought out at the proper moment." She buzzed away, shaking her head as she flew.

"What's her problem?" Henny asked me. "An emerald's a rock, right?"

"Strictly speaking, yes," I agreed. "Maybe we better refer to it as an emerald from here on out. We want her to be generous when the time comes."

Henny agreed, and we faded into the background to study the newly arriving guests.

Everybody had dolled up for this shindig. Long, colorful gowns and drab, black tuxedos ruled the day. All at once, a swirl of raucous laughter sounded, and six young men, one in a white-jacketed tuxedo, rolled into the room, raising the noise level by a function of about a hundred. The fellow in the white jacket cut off from the others and walked up to Arabella to deliver a kiss on the cheek. Arabella resembled a block of ice, the peck on the cheek the merest dab of sunlight. No defrosting occurred.

"He must be the fiancé," I said to Henny.

"She doesn't seem to take to him much."

The young man said a few words to Arabella, whose eyes went to the other men, then back to him, finally settling into a disapproving glare. Her only concession to animation was to tilt her head back slightly as if the scene could better be observed if viewed down the bridge of her nose. The young man rejoined his buddies, already clustered near the bar laughing and pointing at bottles. Henny tapped my arm. "They don't much look like guys who'd be awed by the beauty of a priceless, heirloom emerald sitting on a bed of diamonds."

"No, not unless they're jewel thieves…"

Henny's eyes met mine, and I said, "You don't think the old lady's wary of them, do you?"

"Hard to see how they could pull off a heist here." Henny swept the room with his right arm. "But let's go ask her."

We loitered around Arabella until she got free for a moment from greeting her guests.

"Mrs. von Schneiderhoven," I beckoned.

"What, what, what?" she snapped.

"Mr. Henny and I wondered whether you have any suspicions about the noisy group of guests who arrived…" I couldn't even finish my question.

"Suspicions! Leonard's friends…they're impossible! Loud, crude. Life's a big joke to them. How Ariadne ever met such a crew…" Arabella flapped her arms in frustration. "What can I do? Leonard is the only man ever willing to marry Ariadne. She has to marry someone. She can't mope around the house until she's an old maid, can she?"

Arabella seemed to want an answer to her rhetorical question, so I said, "No, we wouldn't want that."

"No, we wouldn't. Her *father's* no help." Arabella's glance went to an old man with sparse white hair and a white mustache, sitting on a soft chair across the room, his head tilted sideways, his mouth hanging open. A half-filled tumbler of something brown teetered in his right hand, which balanced precariously atop the chair arm. "That man sleeps more than a cat. Yes, watch them. Watch everyone."

Arabella appeared near her breaking point, so I changed the topic.

"Where is your daughter?" I asked.

At that moment, a bright smile burst forth on Arabella's face.

"There's my precious." Arabella scurried off toward a newly-arrived, younger, taller version of herself clad in a violet gown showing considerable décolletage. Ariadne, for sure. Ariadne's hair stood rolled into a tower stretching maybe a foot above her head, giving her the appearance of a fairy tale giantess.

"Sweet Jesus," I heard Henny say.

Rather than have Henny and me there to protect an emerald we hadn't even yet seen, Arabella should have hired us to locate her daughter's jaw, because she didn't have one. The woman's lower lip slid back and immediately became part of her neck. Her upper lip curled toward the tip of her nose. She had the largest ears I'd ever seen. I swear, you could have launched her off a fifty-story building and watching her sail gracefully to the ground. In fact, she could have changed the direction of her glide by simply turning her head from right to left.

"What do you think?" I asked Henny.

"I think she must come with a dowry the size of her boobs."

"That'd be an awful lot of money," I answered.

"Would take an awful lot of money to unload her."

Ariadne accepted the attentions of her guests, a crooked smile on her face. Henny and I drifted back toward the bar. We knew we couldn't drink, but the bar seemed an unobtrusive spot to idle. Not drinking would have been tougher if they'd stocked Boone's That's All, but they didn't. Rich people couldn't have everything, I realized, with some satisfaction.

The raucous six lifted their first drinks of the day in a toast to their newly engaged pal, who accepted their worship with unbecoming immodesty. Finally, Leonard noticed his beloved, and the raucous six became the raucous five as Leonard stepped briskly across the room. Ariadne extended two hands toward Leonard, who grasped them and stretched up to peck her cheek. I watched Ariadne's eyes stare out above Leonard's shoulder toward his five gentleman friends. Perhaps she disapproved of them, too.

Henny tapped his wrist. "I think my watch stopped. I better stop looking at her. My arteries will go next."

"Stop it," I scolded. "We have work to do."

"Would you marry Susan for love or Ariadne for more money than you'd ever need?"

"Detection, not philosophy, okay. We're working here."

The party soon recovered from Ariadne's arrival, even if Henny couldn't. Ariadne went over to the raucous five to greet them. When Leonard stepped away to get her a drink, Ariadne whispered something into the ear of one of the five friends, and they laughed. Leonard returned with the drink and took his sweetheart away, the raucous five hefting their glasses to him again, this time with a shout of encouragement as he went. To pass the time and wary of our names not being on any of the place cards, whenever a waiter carried an hors d'oeuvres-filled tray past us, Henny and I grabbed something. At the end of an hour, a tinkling bell called everyone to their places at the table. Arabella approached Henny and me.

"I will bring out the emerald after dinner. You may sit over there and eat."

She pointed to a small, square table for two to the right of the bar next to the window.

"The children's table," Henny muttered. We took our places and had a terrific dinner—more things than I can describe. Henny and I had snacked considerably, though, and couldn't eat much after the fourth course. But what we ate was fabulous. Wineglasses were conspicuously missing from our table, nor were we permitted to participate in the toast given by one of the raucous five. The cost of being professional.

The dinner went on forever as course after course came marching in from the kitchen. One self-identified old aunt gave a touching narrative of helping to raise Ariadne, complete with a report of measles, mumps, chicken pox, and her first bra—a blood-curdling example of TMI, if ever there was one. I saw Henny glance with longing at the table full of booze and couldn't blame him one little bit.

Night had fallen by the time the help cleared the dining table of the dinner debris. People knew what came next, and I could feel the excitement building. Surprisingly, Arabella beckoned Henny and me. In a voice calculated to be overheard she said, "Go with Osgood and bring the emerald." A woooo went through the crowd.

Henny and I followed butler Osgood out of the room and up the wide, winding stairs into an office. Osgood opened a safe and took out a tiny ring box. We made an about face and followed butler Osgood back into the ballroom. The drapes were drawn across the room-wide windows behind the bar, the chandelier lit but not very brightly, and the room looked cozy, though hazy shadows lurked in the corners. Osgood handed the ring box to Arabella, who faced her guests, clustered around the end of the table nearest the room's entry doors.

"My darling Ariadne has found the man of her dreams," she began but paused to glare hatefully when the raucous five began to hoot. "Excuse me," she chided coldly. The raucous five bowed their heads at the rebuke, and when Leonard, who stood alongside Ariadne at her mother's shoulder, waved nervously toward them, they dutifully dispersed into the background.

"I was saying," Arabella continued snootily, "Leonard will cherish and care for my baby girl..."

"Baby elephant," Henny whispered in my ear. "Baby circus freak."

I jabbed Henny as Arabella droned on.

"...and Ariadne will do the same in return."

The old aunt who'd delivered the stirring biography gave a sentimental series of sniffs. When her sniffling died down, Arabella placed the ring box down on the table.

"This exquisite, gold ring—a beautiful Columbian emerald set on a bed of diamonds—will be a symbol of their love as it has been a symbol of the love Archibald and I have felt for so many years."

Archibald heard his name and raised his glass.

"Married forever," he cried. Forever came out "foreber," but he'd made his paternal contribution to the ceremony.

Arabella set her jaw and finished up.

"This beautiful gem will outlive, but not outshine, their love."

Arabella opened the box and set it on the table as her oohing and aahing guests crowded in. Henny and I crowded in, too. There it sat in its little ring-box slot, magnificent even in the dim light of the gigantic chandelier. Suddenly, the lights went out, and a cacophony of surprised yelps commenced. Ariadne caterwauled above the mayhem, her voice ringing out her distress.

Shouts of "What happened to the lights?" "Get the lights!" and things of that nature echoed through the dark room. People shuffled about, spinning in confusion.

Above the din, even over the voice of a distraught Ariadne, came Mrs. von Schneiderhoven's bellow.

"Osgood, get those lights back on."

An instant later, the chandelier bloomed with illumination. Osgood stood by the open doorway, his finger on the light switch. A scream of shock brought me back to the emerald ring on the table. But the ring wasn't on the table; only the jewel box sat there, empty and alone in all of its sad glory.

Nine

The burst of light revealed Ariadne staggering left and right in a swoon. Arabella lifted her arm like Moses parting the Red Sea and pointed to the two sliding entry doors.

"Osgood!" she screeched. "Close those doors." She stomped her way to within two inches of Leonard. "Explain this!"

Ariadne let out a wail of horrified agony. "No, no, no," she cried repeatedly.

"Ariadne, control yourself," her mother ordered. "Sit her down."

One of the raucous five, along with the biographical aunt and Henny, took the grieving Ariadne by the elbows and guided her out of the crowded muddle of guests to a soft chair near her father. Henny diverged from the procession halfway to the chair and took a step toward the bar. He stood still and simply stared at the arrangement of booze laid out. Ariadne reached her chair and with a final, sad cry of disappointment, slumped back, to all eyes, heartbroken.

Her father's eyes opened. He lifted his glass and cried, "Married forever." He leaned back and closed his eyes.

Henny rejoined me as Arabella started in on Leonard.

"This is a prank by one of your friends, but I do not find it amusing."

"No, no. They wouldn't." Leonard looked plaintively at his five buddies, standing in a cluster, worried looks on their faces. "Would you?"

A muttering, mumbling denial issued en masse.

"I don't believe you. I don't believe them," Arabella ranted. "This is exactly something your idiot friends would think funny. Something you would think funny."

The well-heeled guests stood mute watching the drama unfold. Arabella grabbed the ring box from the table, snapped it closed, and walked to the nearest of the raucous five.

"Take this," she ordered.

The dazed young man took the box.

Arabella's voice sank low. "I am going to have Osgood turn out the lights. Whichever of you mor…gentlemen is playing this joke is behaving in extremely poor taste. When the room is dark, pass the box from one to the other of you. Whichever of you took the ring, open the box, insert the ring, close the top, and no one will ever know who committed this atrocity. You…" She pointed to the man nearest Leonard. "…pass the box to him. Put the box on the table, Leonard. Tell me when it's there, and I will have the lights turned on. Osgood!"

The poor fellow with the empty ring box gazed at Leonard, stupefied. Then everyone stood in darkness. No one made a sound. I strained my ears, trying to hear the hinges of the ring box open and close, but I heard nothing. I made a note to ask Henny whether the Green Hornet ever lived through something like this.

"I've placed the box on the table." Leonard's voice.

"Osgood!" The room lit.

There sat the ring box, the observed of all observers. Arabella took two steps toward the table and picked up the box. She flipped it open. Empty still! Another explosion of guest babble broke the silence. I kept my eye on Arabella as her lower jaw trembled. The look on her face quieted everyone. Slowly, precisely, she spoke.

"I want each of you…gentlemen…to empty your pockets on the table. This includes you, Leonard."

A screech of sad disbelief came from the distant Ariadne followed by a faint, "Oh, Leo, how could you?" and an even fainter, more distant, "Married foreber."

"How could I?" Leonard blurted as if his voice had just sat on a hot stove. "How could I what? I didn't do anything."

Arabella interrupted.

"I do not want to call the police. I do not want to have the five of you arrested. I do not want the name of von Schneiderhoven in the newspapers."

I thought of Susan. What a story for her!

"Empty your pockets, your cuffs, your wallets. I will strip you naked if I have to."

One of the raucous five took the dare and moved up to the dining table.

"I don't care a fig. I have nothing to hide." He turned every pocket he had inside out. He took off his shoes and socks. Then his jacket, pants and shirt. Then his undershirt.

"I presume I may stop here," he said. "Unless you would like to continue the search in another room, Mrs. von Schneiderhoven." He grabbed himself by the butt cheeks and jumped up and down. "But I assure you, you will find nothing."

"Put your clothes back on, young man," Arabella ordered.

I imagined the man shamed her into ceasing her investigation, but no.

"Each of you now, do exactly what that young man did. If one of you falters, you will be arrested, if I have anything to do with it, and I will have a lot to do with it. Police Chief O'Malley is a personal friend of mine."

One by one, the striptease repeated, along with the pogo stick ending. It revealed nothing except for exposing one of the raucous five's odd affection for cartoon characters on his briefs.

"Now you, Leonard," said Arabella.

Leonard gasped.

Henny tapped me, and we slid away. He led me to the bar and grabbed two small, cylindrical glasses, each having a short stem and circular base.

"What's this for?" I asked.

Henny took the full bottle of *crème de menthe* and poured us each a glassful.

"Drink," he ordered. He threw his head back, and emptied the glass. He shook his head, grimaced, and blinked his eyes repeatedly. Then he held the bottle up to the light and poured himself another. "I said drink. Trust me."

I sipped. "Gaaa! It tastes like melted leprechaun. God, it's so sweet."

Henny threw back his second glass and held out the bottle to me.

"What are we doing?" I challenged.

Henny's eyes went blank for a moment.

"Drink it. Hurry up."

I finished my glass in three repulsive sips. Henny poured himself another.

"Have you gone nuts?" I cried.

"I read…I read…" He downed half of his drink. "1940s' novel. Can't remember which one. Published by the Mystery League. Thief hid the stolen emerald in a…hic…"

"In a hick? What's a hick?"

Henny downed the rest of his drink, held the diminishing contents of the bottle to the light, and poured himself another.

"Hid the emerald where? No, I'm not drinking any more of that congealed shamrock juice."

"Hid the emerald in a bottle of *crème de menthe*!"

"What!"

"Or maybe it was a ruby in a bottle of port wine. Whatever."

I grabbed the bottle to prevent Henny from pouring himself a fifth drink, went behind the bar, and poured the green liquor slowly and carefully into the vat of ice, watching for anything remotely resembling a ring to come tumbling out of it. Nothing but green sweetness issued forth.

"Why'd you have to drink it? You only needed to pour it out. You're going to be sick."

"Hic." Henny stared at me as if we'd only just met. "Urp! In the story, the detective calmly drank *crème de menthe* or port or something while he chatted with the thief—tormenting the thief as the stuff in the bottle got lower and lower. It was a great…"

Henny's stomach exploded and with a loud retching sound, the *crème de menthe* Henny had imbibed was no longer imbibed but rather sprayed across the bar and the floor in front of the bar. I saw Leonard putting his pants back on as the crowd turned toward the new disruption. A gasp of disgust overwhelmed their interest in the missing emerald for a moment. Ariadne rose from her chair and approached, her face contorted into revulsion, her hand clasped to her stomach to prevent her own retching at the sight.

"What did he do? Oh, my goodness. I'll get some paper towels." She looked at me. "You're his friend. You can clean this up."

I had no intention of doing any such thing, and when Ariadne reappeared through the open entry doors toting a roll of paper towels, I headed for the hills.

Having purged his system, Henny felt much better. He took the paper towels from Ariadne and ripped off a few to dab at his shirt front. He scattered some loose towels on the floor mess before setting the roll of towels on the bar and walking over to me as if nothing had happened.

Arabella had resumed center stage.

"I hope not to have to call in the police. Fortunately, I have two of New York City's very best professional investigators here tonight." For a moment I felt the excitement of getting to meet them, then everyone turned toward Henny and me as Henny finished cleaning the *crème de menthe* mixed with his digestive juices off his shirt front.

Arabella rolled forward, a battleship ready to engage. "Do something, the two of you. I'm not paying you anything unless and until I have my ring back." Guests spread out in small groups to discuss the problem.

"The ring wasn't in the *crème de menthe*," Henny assured her.

"What? What is he babbling about?" Arabella fumed.

"Do you think one of your guests might have taken the ring?" I asked.

"Do I think…? Yes, I think one of my guests stole the ring. Of course I do. What kind of a question is that? The ring's gone, isn't it? Think. You were here. Where were people standing? Who could have possibly done this?"

Henny and I stood mute as daffodils.

Henny tried. "If your son-in-law to be…"

"He's not my son-in-law to be, and he never will be. Somehow it's him. Or one of his idiot gaggle of friends."

"You searched everyone," Henny finished. "If Leonard and his friends are clean, it has to be someone else."

"They are not clean," Arabella growled. "They did it. One of them did it. Find out who. Under no circumstances will I search my friends. Why the very idea…" She stormed away.

After making a speech in which she promised to contact Chief O'Malley informally, Arabella sent everyone home. Henny and I had expected to stay the night, but when Arabella confronted us after her speech and said, "You, too," there went that. She did, at least, have the driver get us back to Williamsburg after we pleaded with him en route not to drop us off at our office.

"How do you feel?" I asked Henny as we slogged up the dank stairway to our apartments.

"Did I really throw up all over the place?"

"You did. But at least you proved the emerald wasn't in the *crème de menthe*."

Our eyes met, and we burst into laughter. If that could be called a happy ending, then the day had had a happy ending.

I lay in bed next morning, regurgitating everything that happened after the lights went out, but I could see no better in the bright light of the new day in my apartment than I saw in the deep darkness of Arabella's ballroom the evening before. Somebody snatched the emerald ring. Obvious. The guests were clustered near the butt of the table where the ring sat. Anyone could have made a lightning strike and pocketed the bauble. Anyone but the raucous six, who'd been stripped nearly naked and bounced by Arabella. No other guest had been searched, and now they'd dispersed to the four winds. My cell played its tune, and I said hello to Susan.

"Guess what?" she bubbled. "The *Post* called me in for an interview Monday morning, tomorrow morning, at ten. Isn't that great?"

"How was your date?"

"My date? Meh. Who cares about my date? Isn't it exciting?"

I roused myself, knowing self-pity would not become me.

"Great news. Anything from the *Times* or *Daily News*?"

"No. But one of the big three isn't bad."

"Not bad at all; you're right. What did the person say?"

"Molly. Her name was Molly. She complimented me on the election story, of course, and said she wanted to meet me. Oh, how I wish I had more to give her than the *World Journal* and a college degree."

You can guess what immediately crossed my mind. I had a great story for Susan and said so.

"What kind of story?"

After swearing Susan to secrecy off the record or background—I tossed in every word I'd ever heard associated with keeping things out of the newspapers—I went over the previous day in detail, only leaving out Henny's floor show with the *crème de menthe* bottle.

"Let me go now and write everything down for my own memory. I promise not to publish anything, but I can use this in my interview, can't I? Say it's a story I'm working on?"

"As long as nothing gets out."

Henny and I sat at our desks early Monday afternoon, morose. Henny hadn't tossed his fedora at the coat rack even once, a sure sign of depression. I'd thought for a moment of having a bottle of *crème de menthe* waiting on his desk for him, but finally, couldn't see the humor in it, and if I didn't think it was funny, I doubted whether Henny would.

A quick knock at the door produced Susan. I'd mentioned Susan's interview to Henny. His response: "I'm glad someone's getting ahead in the world."

"How'd it go?" I asked as Susan sat in our client chair. She lifted her feet from the floor and spun around in a circle twice.

"That's how it went!" she cried. "She hired me! An investigative reporter! I am an investigative reporter! I start in two weeks. Takes that long for the paperwork to go through, according to Molly. You have to finish this emerald case. You have to find the ring. What's your plan?"

"What do you care?" Henny asked in a glum tone.

"Molly loved hearing I was at work on another hot story. She's heard of your Mrs. von Schneiderhoven. She wants the *Post* to have the story of the theft exclusively." Susan made another double orbit with the chair. "Your plan. Your plan. What's your plan?"

Both Henny and I spread our hands wide.

"What's that mean?" Susan asked, her brow furrowing, her chair grinding to a halt.

I explained. "Mrs. Schneiderhoven hates us. She's not paying us. The whole thing is an unsolvable puzzle and a total waste of time."

"No, no, no," Susan disagreed. "This is important. You have to find that emerald ring," Susan insisted. "One of those friends of the groom must have taken it."

"He's not a groom nor is he ever likely to be a groom— certainly not Ariadne's groom," Henny said.

"No one else could have taken the ring," Susan argued. "Do you remember anybody being near the table?"

"Everybody was near the table," Henny explained.

"Didn't either of you feel someone move toward the table?" Susan asked.

"There was a lot of milling when the lights went out—milling and shouting. We might accurately call it chaos," I said. "Anyone could have sidled up to the table." I checked with Henny.

"He's right. No one would have noticed unless they got knocked over."

"Did you question Leonard's friends?" Susan asked.

"We didn't question anybody," I said. "Arabella ran the show."

"Then it's time for the two of you to do some investigating. You are detectives, aren't you? Your window sign says so." Susan pointed.

"Henny and I can't call Arabella for a guest list," I said. "She'd hang up…" I snapped my fingers. "…like this. So would everybody else in the house, I'm sure."

"What's Leonard's last name?" Susan asked.

Henny and I shrugged, and Susan rolled her eyes.

"Don't call Arabella, then," she said. "Call the butler or Ariadne. Get Leonard's last name and phone number from one of them. Then call Leonard and get the others' numbers and names and go to work on them!"

"Spade and Marlowe wouldn't sit and mope," Henny said, glancing my way.

"Neither would the Green Hornet," I tossed back at him. When a look of befuddlement crossed Susan's face, I regretted the reference. "But who can we call to get Leonard's info?"

"Our driver!" Henny cried.

Arabella had rented the fellow who drove us to and fro, and the driver had given us his card in case we ever needed limousine transportation again—a very unlikely possibility, it seemed to me. Henny dug the card out of his wallet and made the call.

Turns out Amirani Slogovian had driven Leonard out to Ariadne's place numerous times, and after Henny promised to direct all of our travel business his way, Amirani gave us the young man's cell number and work address.

Susan clapped her hands, congratulated us on a successful first step, gave me a hug, and left to go start the final two weeks of her *World Journal* reporting.

"Nice dame," Henny complimented.

I agreed with Henny a hundred percent.

Henny punched in Leonard's number, and we launched our investigation.

Ten

Leonard professed relief at hearing from Henny and me—two professionals who could help him, or so he said over speakerphone. He repeated his pleas of innocence with a passion not easily dismissed. Ariadne no longer accepted his phone calls, he told us, and unfriended him on Facebook. (Henny and I had talked about creating a presence on Facebook, but with the concept being so far removed from the 1940s, and with a firm belief Spade and Marlowe would have mocked him for such behavior, Henny resisted.)

We commiserated with Leonard on his loss and hung up to await his promised email with the names and numbers of his five friends. This much technology, Henny would permit. When the email arrived, Henny grabbed two names, and I grabbed two. I know that doesn't add up to five, but it did. Francis Ingraham Rightman; Michael Steward David; Gregory J Wasserbrickle; and two brothers who ran a computer store, Tom and Tim Vokalas.

I took the Wasserbrickle guy. How could a fellow with a name like that not be interesting? He sold cars—used cars—and his eyes lit up when I entered his lot looking about me with an eager eye. He bustled over and stopped abruptly when he recognized me.

"Hey, you were at the party on Saturday. One of Mrs. von Schneiderhoven's watchdogs."

"I was." I had my spiel all ready. "Leonard wants all of his friends cleared beyond any suspicion, so he wants us to track down the ring. I think we can all agree it's got to be somewhere."

Gregory thrust out his two hands as if preparing to play the piano.

"No rings on me."

I nodded. "Can you tell me anything about the night? Any theories you might have about where the ring disappeared to, Mr. Wasserbrickle?"

"Come on inside. Call me Greg."

I followed Greg into a trailer/office. He poured us each a cup of coffee and chased his only other salesman out onto the lot. With this preparation, I hoped for a revelation. No such luck.

"I have no idea," he said and sipped from his cup. "We were there to cheer Leo on. He'd found himself a miracle girl; then the lights went out along with his dreams."

"Did you notice anyone move toward the table when the lights went?"

"Did I notice in the dark?"

"Well, did you feel anyone move toward the table?"

"Nope, not specifically toward the table. People were moving around, though. Somebody screamed, Ariadne, I think. As I said, there was lots of shuffling around, but I couldn't say anyone pushed me out of the way to get to the ring, or anything like that. Just confusion for the moment. The lights came on and…mystery!"

"How long have you known Ariadne?"

"Leo sells furniture. He sold some to Ariadne about six months ago. He saw what she bought—a lot. An expensive lot. He noticed where she lived. An expensive address. He rode out in the truck to deliver the furniture. He wanted to make sure his imagination matched reality, he told us. He helped Ariadne with the furniture arrangement, all bedroom furniture, by the way. He liked what he saw; he dated her; he chased her; he caught her."

"What was it he about her he liked?"

"Her looks." Here, Greg burst out into uncontrollable laughter.

"Her money?" I asked when he had his breath back.

"Ya think?"

"He'd live with her for the rest of his life just to get her money?"

"Well, she does have a set of knockers, and you know what they say."

"What do they say?"

"In the dark, all women are beautiful." Greg ripped off another peal of laughter.

"Did you fellows joke about their…relationship? Did Leo think it was a joke?"

"We did, and, sure, Leo joined in. He knew what he was doing and what he was getting. The cost and the value."

"And everybody joked about it?"

"Sure. Well, not so much Frankie."

"Frankie would be Francis Rightman?" He was the other name on my list.

"Yeah."

"Go on. He didn't joke because…?"

Greg shrugged. "I got the impression he didn't think it was so funny. He did at first, but I guess he grew a conscience. He even left the bar one night when we were cracking wise about Ariadne. Never argued with us or anything, but, yeah, now you make me think about it, he really was an outlier on this."

A question arose in my detective mind, and I immediately complimented myself for my perspicacity.

"Would he have been the fellow who helped Ariadne to a seat after the lights came on?"

Greg leaned his head back and closed his eyes.

"Yes, yes he was, now you mention it. Not surprising, though, after what—you know—I just told you."

"No, not surprising at all." I stood. Then I recalled Ariadne whispering briefly into this same fellow's ear and their both laughing. "If anything pops into your head, here's my card. Let me know. Leonard's worried about you guys."

"I will, yeah. Thanks."

I bid Greg farewell and set out after Frankie.

According to Leonard, Frankie worked as a salesman in his father's real estate concern. I found the Rightman real estate office on the second floor of the Twenty-Third Street address Leonard'd given me. There were two desks and an inner office door. A young woman sat at one desk, looking down at her cell phone.

"Excuse me. I'm looking for Francis Rightman."

"Senior or junior?" Henny would have loved this woman. She had puffy blonde hair, chewed gum, and wore a button-up sweater along with a pair of glasses having sharp, sweeping, upper corners, attached to a neck strap.

"The junior, I suppose."

"I'll ask," she said in a whiny, nasal voice. She got up and swayed her way into the inner office. A moment later a large man in a black suit, tie loosened at the collar, hair disheveled, burst out.

"Do you know where he is?" the man growled.

"Know…who?"

"My son. He didn't showed up for work today, and he's got three clients on his list to show around. Won't answer my calls."

"No, I don't know. I'm looking for him, too."

The elder Francis ran his hand through his hair and took a deep breath.

"Can I help you?" he asked with barely contained patience.

"Have you spoken to him since Saturday?"

"No."

"Well, sorry then, I don't think you can help me. Oh, do you know either of two women named Ariadne von Schneiderhoven or Arabella von Schneiderhoven?"

"Schneider-whaten? They looking for an apartment?"

"No, no. They live in a very nice home on Long Island."

"Give them my card. Maybe I can help them. You never know." Francis senior handed me his card.

"I'll do that. Do you know them? Ever heard of them?"

"No. Anything else?"

I felt silly digging in my coat pocket for my card and handing it over to him—like we were businessmen networking—but it was the only thing I could think of to do. Frankie senior took the card and frowned.

"What's this? Private eye?"

"If your son shows up, can you have him call me?"

"What's it about? He in any trouble?"

"No, of course not. There was an incident he witnessed the other night, and I simply want to get his take on it."

Frankie senior nodded as if he didn't believe me, and I made my exit.

I spent the rest of the day in the office not doing much. Susan called once and asked how Henny and I were progressing. I told her I was waiting for Henny to return, and she promised she'd come by the office when she finished up with her *World Journal* day. At the moment, she was covering the opening of a new Dim Sum parlor on Pell Street. She promised to bring some samples.

When Henny showed up, he and I compared notes. His report was distressingly brief.

"The two brothers knew nothing. Michael David, he knew even less. Leonard often invited them places. He invited them to the party. They liked parties, so they went. They all agreed the stretch limo ride was more fun than the party."

"Did they mention anything funny about Francis Rightman?"

"Funny? What do you mean funny?"

I explained about Rightman's tepid championing of Ariadne's honor.

Henny looked thoughtful. "Michael David did say how much they mocked Leonard, and Leonard didn't mind it. Even got off a good one on himself once in a while. The two brothers admitted they were surprised when Francis showed up in the limo Saturday night.”

“Why?”

Henny shrugged. “Just surprised he’d be interested. Oh, and he didn’t drink on the trip out, they said. The car had a bar in back where they sat, but he’s the only one who didn’t drink. Surprised the brothers ’cause he always drank when they were together. He wouldn’t even toast Ariadne the many times everyone toasted her on the trip out.”

“Everybody acknowledged Leonard was chasing the money, not Ariadne?”

“Sure. Michael David still laughed about it. Gotta take the good with bad, he said. Thought it was hilarious.”

Susan walked in, bakery box in hand.

“Hello, gentlemen. Leftovers. Dig in. Have you found the emerald?”

Henny and I filled Susan in, alternating our reporting as we munched on buns.

“Francis Rightman seems to be the anomaly,” Susan said. “You know—what doesn’t belong in this picture?”

“We know what an anomaly is,” I said, frowning my resentment toward Susan’s condescension.

Susan gave a giggle, and my heart twittered.

“And Ariadne unfriended her beau on Facebook? Seems a trite thing to do. Let’s look on Facebook. Open up your page,” Susan ordered.

“Well,” I said slowly, “neither of us has a page.”

“Everybody’s on Facebook! Your private eye establishment should be on Facebook.”

"It's a little too modern for Henny," I explained.

"Henny, tsk tsk," Susan scolded, shaking her head. "I'll look from my page."

Susan got our computer going and did what she had to do.

"Come see this," she said.

Henny and I bent over her shoulders.

"This is Ariadne von Schneiderhoven's page. See?"

Susan pointed to three photographs of Ariadne and the raucous six. She enlarged one of the photos. They stood in a garden, Ariadne front and center, Leonard to her right, his arm around her waist.

"Look, can you see that?" Susan asked, touching the screen.

Henny and I leaned in. There were two hands resting on Ariadne's left hip, and unless Leonard had two left arms, the second arm belonged to someone else. And the only person whose arm and hand it could be, studying the geometry of the photo, was Francis Ingraham Rightman.

"You fellows have to get yourselves on Facebook," Susan advised. "I don't see how you can investigate people without it. More to the point; why is this Rightman sneaking his arm around Ariadne? Look, she posted the photo only a week ago."

Henny and I went back to our chairs, and Susan returned to our client chair.

"Rightman helped her to her chair that night when the ring disappeared," I said. "And I remember her looking over Leonard's shoulder at the five friends when he greeted her with a hug and kiss on Saturday. Can't say if she was looking at anyone specifically, though. They also spoke for a brief moment, Rightman and her."

"And Francis Rightman didn't go to work today?" Susan asked, looking for confirmation.

I confirmed the fact.

"Something's not right here," she decided.

Henny spoke up. "Lloyd, you think we could get in to talk with Ariadne?"

"Out on Long Island?"

"Of course."

"No, but let me call and ask, anyway."

I tapped in the number Arabella left with us, and Osgood answered. He promised to check with "Madam" and call right back. He did. He said Ariadne was out, but it didn't matter. The "madam" had banned us.

"Hmmm," Susan hummed thoughtfully. "Ariadne's out and Francis Rightman didn't go into work today. Suspicious, eh?"

"You should have said we have news about the ring," Henny reasoned. "Then she'd have gotten on the phone."

"We don't have news about the ring," I argued.

"The old lady doesn't know that," Henny argued back.

"I'll go," Susan offered. "I'll phone the von Schneiderhovens tomorrow morning so they don't link your call with mine. I'll say I work for the *Post*, and I'll make up a story about the *Post* wanting to do a puff piece on the family. I'll research them on Facebook, Henny, and see what I can use. Maybe they're philanthropists or animal lovers or vegetarians. I'll find something. And you two get on Facebook. I'll call you tomorrow."

Henny and I went home feeling none too good that evening. The next workday passed with no news and quiet desperation on Henny's and my part. We tossed a few ideas back and forth, but all of our ideas piled in a heap amounted to useless. After a dinner of lo mein noodles, I lay in bed replaying every moment of Arabella's party I could recall. Then, at about nine o'clock, my cell phone chimed.

"It's me," came Susan's voice. "I don't have time to talk, but you'll be getting two guests at your office some time tomorrow. Make certain you're there. Don't leave your office empty for a moment. And be sure Henny's with you. And above all; don't mention anything about me. Got it?"

"I got it, but who's visiting?"

Susan laughed. "Be there." She ended the call.

I went down three flights to Henny's apartment and knocked on his door.

He opened it, wearing blue silk pajamas.

"Where'd you get those?"

"William Powell wore them in one of the *Thin Man* movies."

I considered. "How do you know they were blue in a black and white movie?"

"Nora said. Anyway, these were on sale. What do you care? What's up?"

I explained.

"She didn't say who the visitors were? New clients, maybe?" Henny suggested.

"Nothing."

"This is great. So *noir*."

I stared at Henny. So *noir*?

"Sounds like the start of a Sam Spade story. Okay, I'll be in the office early. See you tomorrow."

Henny and his blue pajamas closed the door.

Eleven

Henny and I hung around the office next morning, Henny doing practice tosses of his hat at the coat rack, me too nervous to read, pacing back and forth a great deal and looking out of the window for our guests. Neither one of us wanted to leave and get some lunch, but we flipped a coin and I lost, so I hurried across the street and brought back pizza without missing anything. Come to think of it, I'd lost two coin tosses to Henny recently. I made a note to look into it.

A little before two o'clock, our door opened slowly, and there stood Ariadne, her hair still piled up on her head, dressed in a short fur jacket over a long yellow dress. She had yet to acquire a chin. When she stepped into the office, Henny tapped his wristwatch as if it had stopped. Then he put it to his ear. What a character. I decided I'd better take the lead.

"What can we do for you, Ms. von Schneiderhoven?"

"He…and it…will be here in a moment. I hoped he might precede me. Let it be understood that word of this cannot leave this room. Swear it, or I leave right now."

Henny and I gave what I knew Henny would describe as a "furtive glance" toward one another.

"You have our word," Henny promised. He gestured. "Please, sit."

Ariadne commandeered our client chair.

"We'll wait for him."

Neither Henny nor I wished to display any ignorance about the situation, so we shut up. Ten excruciating minutes later, I detected the faint clanging of our elevator, and a moment afterward, Ariadne got to her feet and went to answer the tap on the door. Francis Ingraham Rightman took two steps inside, put his arm around Ariadne, and proceeded toward our desks.

"Give it to him," Ariadne ordered.

Frankie reached into his pocket and pulled out some wadded tissue. He placed it on Henny's desk. Henny unwrapped it, and there it was—the Columbian emerald in a gold ring on a bed of diamonds, ready for whoever's finger would claim it. Henny rewrapped the ring and put it into his top drawer. Ariadne drew her head back and gave an order.

"You will return it to my mother without mentioning either me or Francis. This is to ensure your silence." Ariadne carried a small handbag. From it she took a check she'd filled out earlier and handed it to Frankie, who handed it to Henny, who handed it to me. Five thousand dollars.

"I control some of my own fortune, and I consider this money well-spent. Francis and I plan to be married eventually, and there must be no cloud over us. Do you understand?"

Since Ariadne believed Henny's and my understanding to be worth five thousand dollars, we both professed to understand. Entirely.

"Then we can leave, darling," Ariadne said.

"One thing," Henny blurted. "Please. How did you end up with this ring?"

When Ariadne and her beau appeared reluctant, Henny said, "We know you took the ring. What can it hurt to let us know how? We're naturally curious."

"Well… You tell them, darling," Ariadne said.

"Everyone stood around the table, you'll recall. When Leonard waved us off after Mrs. Schneiderhoven expressed her unhappiness with our behavior, I moved away from the table along with the others. Everybody, even Osgood, wanted to see the ring, and no one noticed me take those few extra steps toward the door and douse the lights. Ariadne screamed when the lights went out and kept screaming so I could find my way back to the table. She also staggered back and forth and all around, so if I banged into anyone on my way back to the table to snatch the ring, it wouldn't be noticed as much. Turns out, everybody was moving around. I shouldered at least four people, but no one thought anything of it." He gave a broad smile, and Ariadne leaned in and kissed him. Henny gave a noise of some sort.

"The lights came on. The ring was in my pocket. Ariadne seemed to faint. I helped her to a chair and managed to slide the ring down her top. She sat and watched her mother go through her…investigation."

Ariadne jumped in. "You, Mr. Henny, were very helpful, also."

"Me!"

"Yes, you. You had an incident, you recall?"

In my mind's eye, I saw Henny spraying decorative layers of undigested *crème de menthe* about the place.

"I went for paper towels, you recall—not to help you but to get the ring out of the room. When I got the idea, I stood up but felt the ring slither down my front. I certainly didn't want it to come tumbling out my bottom as if I'd laid an egg. So I clasped my stomach, where the ring had settled, and it appeared as if your…incident made me nauseous. I held the ring in place, left the room, hid the ring until, next day, I got it out of the house."

"And you took the ring because…?" Henny asked.

Ariadne's eyes opened wide. "Anything not to have to get engaged to Leonard. I misjudged him tremendously. But going to my mother and saying I'd changed one man for another, like changing a pair of shoes, no, no. No, no, no! I knew she'd hold Leonard and his friends responsible for the theft. Any hope of a relationship with Leonard would be over. In my own sweet time, I will tell her about Francis." She leaned in and delivered another kiss. Henny repeated the same noise he'd made before. Definitely a gagging sound, which he quickly covered with a cough.

With shining pride Ariadne said, "Francis and I practiced many times for that night. We had more than one option prepared. Now, Mother will be happy at the return of the ring; she'll be happy Leonard is out of the picture—she never liked him, you know—and I am happy with Francis. In time…" She gave Francis a beatific smile. "A wonderful result all around."

I wanted to ask how she expected to get her mother to approve a second member of the raucous six joining the family but chose not to stir up any commotion and jeopardize the fee I expected to get from Arabella. Ariadne's future happiness was Ariadne's problem, not mine.

"Will that be all?" Ariadne asked, not without considerable cockiness on her part.

"Yes," Henny answered. "And may Lloyd and I offer you our sincere congratulations?"

Ariadne and her Francis departed.

"Who makes the call to Arabella?" I asked.

"I will," Henny volunteered. He got Osgood on the line and to preclude any arguing announced right out we'd recovered the ring and needed to speak with Arabella immediately. She came on the line and rejected Henny's offer to drive the ring out to her. She would get in her car immediately and be on the way. We could expect her within two hours, traffic permitting. We shouldn't leave the office. We shouldn't take the ring from the office. We should lock the door of the office and wait for her.

Henny agreed with her demands and both surprised me and raised my admiration for him a couple of notches when he reminded Arabella to bring her checkbook.

A little more than two hours later, like a Mississippi paddle-wheeler announcing itself from around the bend by blowing its steam whistle, Arabella began calling, "Mr. Henny. Mr. Lloyd! Mr. Henny. Mr. Lloyd!" the moment she stepped out of our creaky elevator.

She opened our door without knocking and plowed through the foaming main up to our desks, where she threw down anchor and docked. Henny, the sides of his open, double breasted jacket thrown over the arms of his chair like two flaccid, gigantic bat wings, opened his top desk drawer, drew out the wadded tissue, and revealed the contents.

"Oh, Mr. Lloyd!"

"I'm Henny."

"You've recovered it. You are a miracle worker. How did you do it? Tell me everything." She scooped up the ring, tissue and all, in her paw and shoved the ring deep into the recesses of a black purse she carried. Osgood, by the way, stood at the door. I allowed Henny center stage. He took the toothpick from his mouth and pointed with it at Arabella

"Mr. Lloyd and I worked twenty four-seven, day and night, and at all hours to recover this gem for you, Mrs. von Schneiderhoven. Unfortunately, we cannot go into details. I'm sure you understand. We wouldn't want to put our secret operatives at risk."

Wow! I thought.

A blank look swept over Arabella.

"I do not understand. Who stole it?" she insisted.

"No one you suspected. I can tell you that much," Henny assured her, and for the most part, he told the truth.

"It wasn't one of those friends of Leonard or Leonard himself?"

"No, by no means."

Ariadne's check had worked its magic on Henny. As it should.

"Well!" Arabella huffed. "I don't see how it could have been anyone else. At any rate, I have the ring, and can pass it on to my little girl as soon as she finds a man worthy of her. Not Leonard."

Good luck with that, I thought.

"Osgood!" Arabella barked, adding a wave of her hand.

Osgood walked to Henny and handed him an envelope. After making his delivery, he went and held the door open, and Arabella disappeared from our lives.

"Open it, open it," I urged.

Henny ripped open the envelope and his eyes went wide.

"Fif-teen thou-sand dol-lars!"

"Good lord!" I cried. "Maybe when Ariadne announces her engagement to Francis, we can get hired again to watch over the ring and hope Ariadne changes her mind at the last minute. This could be a growth industry for us, Henny. Let me have it. I'll go deposit both checks now."

I phoned Susan before I left, and when I got back to the office, she already sat in our client's chair.

"Henny's told me everything," she said, a grand smile covering her face.

"How'd you get Ariadne to come in here?" I asked.

"I told her she was a prominent member of society, possibly the subject of a human interest piece by the *Post*."

"Human!" Henny scoffed.

"She invited me out to the house, and we ended up in a girl-to-girl talk. I told her I knew she preferred Francis to Leonard. Wasn't it obvious to the both of you from the Facebook photo and his helping her to the chair after the lights out? Something was up between the two of them."

"I guess," I said.

"At any rate, Ariadne wept, and I soothed her. She wasn't really a thief, she said, and I agreed; neither was Francis, I told her. That sealed the deal, and she admitted to merely wanting to disrupt the evening and get rid of Leonard without looking like a silly idiot to her mother."

Henny scratched his head. "Couldn't she simply go and say 'Mom, I don't like this guy; I like this guy?'"

"No! She said her mother's preparations for the party and for passing on the ring were too far along. Ariadne could not bring herself to incur her mother's opinion that she was…her words…an empty-headed little rich girl who couldn't make up her mind."

"Humph! Does mommy have a surprise coming," I muttered.

"She didn't know how to get the ring back to her mother, and I suggested you gentlemen."

"You are a peach!" Henny lauded.

"So," said Susan, rising, "I have to get back to work, but I have it on good authority the two of you are buying me a real fancy dinner tonight. I've got a place all picked out. Giando on the Water, right over the Williamsburg Bridge in your very own neighborhood. I'm ordering the best, so be prepared. I already made reservations. Meet me there at seven."

Henny stood and got the door for her.

"And you deserve it," he said.

"Go home and freshen up," Susan advised. "Dress up."

I thought we were dressed up, but that's neither here nor there.

Henny went back to his desk.

"Well," he said, "another case we successfully solved."

"Yeah, we. Same as we solved the other two. The less we do, the less we know, the smarter we are. What's wrong with this picture?"

"Works for me," Henny said with a shrug. "Say, you don't think Susan would like to join the firm, do you? She's pretty good at this stuff."

"HENNY, LLOYD AND SUSAN?" I said. "Doesn't sound very *noir* to me."

A stricken look passed over Henny. "No, I guess not. *Noir's* important. But stick with her, Lloyd. She's a keeper."

"You know what we should do?" I asked.

"What?"

"Susan didn't see us in our tuxedos. She said dress up. Let's wear our tuxedos tonight!"

"Great idea!" Henny pulled open his bottom desk drawer and withdrew the box of small paper cups he'd splurged on with a slice of our profits. Out came the Boone's That's All.

"Celebrate the great day and soon-to-be-great dinner?" Henny asked.

"Why not?"

Henny poured.

We drank. Then we drank again.

Twelve

The Rosebud Puzzle

The following Monday, Susan tossed a copy of the *New York Post* on my desk.

"Page six," she said.

I turned to page six. A tasty blurb among a bunch of other blurbs read:

"Henny and Lloyd. Heard of them? A certain party on Long Island is mighty glad she has. They recovered a priceless bauble for her that went missing during a gathering of the moneyed set at a posh Long Island mansion. The party bubbled; the lights went out; the bauble went missing; Henny and Lloyd sprang into action. Bauble returned in a scant few days; all well; happy ending all around."

I handed the paper to Henny.

"It doesn't say very much," I said to Susan. "And you're not mentioned at all."

"My editor explained it. I'm not formally on board the investigative reporting team yet—paperwork still pending—so that sank any byline I could have. And Mrs. von Schneiderhoven promised to sue if the *Post* mentioned her name or anything about her. What you read was the most Molly, my editor, thought the paper could get away with. But Molly gave me my props for getting the story. You're burying the lead, though. The point is, you're mentioned!"

"Yeah, great," I kvetched. "Henny and Lloyd, but no Detective Agency. How's anybody going to know we're for hire? Or that we even exist? Two measly words they couldn't put in there?"

"I complained when I read it, too," Susan explained. "Molly said the paper had a policy about no free ads."

"Two words is a free ad? Everybody will think two lucky schnooks found the emerald in somebody's pants pocket. Nobody will think…"

As if on cue, someone rapped on our office door, and Susan went to get it. A slight, elderly man I recognized as our next door neighbor, the fellow who ran ECHOE LIGHTING, walked in. He carried a newspaper in his right hand. I got a quick look at the headline. Today's *Post*. Henny and I said good morning to him on the elevator and passing in the hall, and he did the same to us, but we'd never formally introduced ourselves. I didn't even know his name. I didn't think it was Echoe.

I rose and circled the desk to shake his hand and motioned him to our client chair.

"I'll be going," Susan said, and go she did.

"I can use your help," the old man said. "I read about you. It is you in the paper, isn't it? I see your sign every day."

"Yes, it is," I assured him. "I'm Lloyd, by the way. He's Henny."

Henny gave a wave, buttoned his black, double-breasted jacket, sat up, and popped a toothpick between his teeth.

"My name is Noah Beamer—Echoe Lighting?"

"Of course, I recognize you," I said. "What can we do for you?"

"My wife passed a week ago."

Henny leaned in. "And you think there was foul play"

Henny was dying to work on a murder case. Me, not so much.

"Foul play?"

"Yeah, you know. Bumped off?"

"What! Oh, no. My goodness, no. She'd been sick. A stroke. Bed-ridden. Mentally…"

Mr. Beamer waffled his hand.

Henny sat back, his disappointment obvious.

"How can we help you?" I asked again.

"I don't know if you can. I hope you can."

Henny removed his toothpick and said, "We won't know until you tell us what it is. Lay it on the line for us."

"Of course. The final week—a very sad week it was, too—the final week, my wife Vicky simply lay there, but every now and then, maybe two, three times a day, she would—energize is the only way I can describe it. She'd energize and say something. Always the same thing, though. That's the puzzling part."

"What did she say?" I asked.

"It wasn't always easy to catch, but it sounded like a little yip of pain and '3-8-13,' and she'd repeat it a few times. Then she'd settle back into a torpor."

"The numbers mean anything to you?" Henny asked.

"No, not a thing. But going through her personal effects—if that's the right term—personal effects?"

"Yes," Henny answered, and he reinserted his toothpick.

"I found this."

Mr. Beamer stood and handed Henny a small, common, rectangular datebook with a picture of daisies on the cover. Henny leafed through it quickly.

"And?" Henny said.

"Look at the back cover. Inside."

Henny did and a look of surprise came over him. He got up and handed me the book.

Hand printed inside the back cover on a line headed "Address" was the notation:

Pa NCHC 19135 3-8-13

It was the only handwritten notation on the page.

"You see the 3-8-13? I'd like to know what it means," Mr. Beamer said. "I'd like to know what Vicky had on her mind so intently in her last hours."

"Do the letters or numbers mean anything to you?" I asked. The puzzle aroused my detective's curiosity. As well it should.

"No, nothing."

I checked the first page of the datebook. "This is from 2009—eight years ago."

Mr. Beamer spread his hands and shrugged.

"I found it," he said lamely.

"Did you find any others?"

"Any other datebooks? No. I've left my store locked. Can I come back after hours? I can pay you for your time if you'll help me with this."

Henny and I looked at one another and saw agreement in each other's eyes.

"Sure," I said. "What time do you close?"

"Six, six-thirty. Organize, lock up. Can we say seven o'clock, here in your office?"

We agreed and Mr. Beamer went back to work.

"What do you think?" I asked Henny.

"Awful lot of numbers. Could be her social security number."

I counted the numbers, and they were the correct amount. I jotted down the possibility.

"Not something I'd be fixated on at my demise," I said. "How about a phone number? It's got the one, and nine-thirteen could be an area code."

"Only five numbers after that, two short for a phone number. Where's nine-thirteen area code?"

I manipulated my cell phone and got the answer.

"Kansas City."

"Kansas City? That doesn't sound useful," Henny said.

"Well, we can suggest it. Maybe Beamer will recognize it as something. What else?"

"Serial number of something she bought?"

I shrugged. "Maybe. But still…thinking about it on her deathbed? How about a license plate?"

"Awfully long for that."

"The Pa at the beginning could be Pennsylvania."

"And the NCHC?"

I took a breath. "I don't know. I got nothing."

"The three-eight-thirteen looks like it could be a date."

"The book's from 2009. The date would have to be 1913 or 2013. I don't think so."

"I guess we'd better ask Susan," Henny suggested.

"Stop! No. No asking Susan. What, are we helpless? We'll figure it out. She already solved two cases for us. Out of three. And the other one, I'm not even sure we solved."

I made two careful copies of the notation and passed one to Henny in case Beamer wanted his wife's book back later.

"Anything else in the book?" Henny asked.

"Yeah. Certain boxes are filled in with stuff she had to do. I'll go through it. You get busy cracking the code."

Nothing got cracked except Henny's knuckles, which he did only when frustrated. I looked carefully through Mrs. Beamer's datebook and found hairdressing appointments, doctors' appointments, meaningless—to me—names of people, usually with a time indicated, I assumed to meet. I checked the date 3-8, but the box was empty, as was the box to its right and the two to its left. But most of the boxes in the book were empty, so that told me nothing except the lady wasn't busy on those days.

I didn't know how long we'd be with Beamer later on, so I suggested Henny go out and bring in some Chinese. He suggested we flip a coin, but I held my ground, pointing out I'd gone out for pizza the day Ariadne brought back the emerald. Plus, I'd gone out for pizza six hours earlier, and I didn't want it again for dinner. Besides, I'd lost those two coin flips recently to Henny and had my suspicions, in a good natured way—you know, heads I win; tails you lose—of Henny's coins.

Henny conceded, and by six forty-five we were fed, had our fortunes revealed to us, and were ready for Beamer, who knocked on the door five minutes early. He didn't recognize the digits as his wife's social security number or as a telephone number. The date 3-8-13 meant nothing to him nor did Kansas City.

"Tell us about your wife," Henny suggested. He stood and took off his jacket, a rare occurrence, and once seated again, grabbed a pen and a pad of paper. I did the same as Mr. Beamer started talking.

"Where to start?" he muttered.

"At the beginning. Don't sugarcoat anything," Henny coaxed as he slid a toothpick between his teeth.

I wondered what 1940s' movie Henny'd stolen sugarcoat out of.

"I met Vicky in 1969 at the Jersey shore. A small town called Margate. You know it? Not too far from Atlantic City."

"Heard of it," I said.

"My friends and I rented a house for the summer of '69. Vicky's friends rented the house next door. Everybody got to know one another, but Vicky was special. Long hair, so pretty. Very hippy-ish. You heard of the 1960s' hippies? Flower power and all of that?"

"I've seen newsreels," Henny answered.

I rolled my eyes. Newsreels. Followed by a short, Chapter 4 of the *Masked Rider*, and two cartoons. And a double feature.

"It was a very fluid summer, if you know what I mean, but Vicky and I stuck. She had nowhere to live. She'd just finished school, a college outside of Philadelphia—Immaculata College, if that helps you. She told me she had an enormous blow-up with her father right after graduation. She left home, crashed with her friends in Margate, then moved right in with me after Labor Day."

"Where were you living then?" I asked.

"Brooklyn. Flatbush. My dad had given me one last summer off before adulthood—he said. I already had my own apartment, thanks to Dad, and I went to work with him in the home furnishing business. There was a lot of building, home building, big apartment buildings going up for a lot of years in Brooklyn, and he did really well. I was in charge of lighting. Then and forever, you see. It wasn't long before Vicky came to work for us as a secretary. My dad liked her. Two years later, we got married. Had one kid, a son. Lives in Idaho. Rarely see him. His moving out west bothered Vicky a lot. Think that might have something to do with…with her dying words?"

I thought of the 3-8-13.

"When did your son move away?" I asked.

"Went to college in Idaho and eventually moved back there. So…2006 he graduated. Came home for a couple years. So, I'd say 2008, late 2008. He'd met a girl during senior year, and they'd been visiting back and forth since then. His leaving for so far away was really the one great sadness in our marriage."

There went my theory the son might have moved away in 2013.

Henny stepped in. He withdrew his toothpick and used it to punctuate his questions.

"So you met your wife in 1969. Where'd she grow up? Why did she leave home? Did she work her whole life? Could she have strayed from the marriage? Was there something hovering over her making her unhappy? Was there anything she regretted? Anything she looked back on fondly? You know, Mr. Beamer…"

"Please call me Noah."

"You know, Noah…" Henny frowned. "…know, Noah, I'm put in mind of *Citizen Kane*. Have you seen the movie? 1941."

Henny gave Noah no time to answer. Now, I'm frowning. What's with all these no nos? At any rate, Henny went on.

"The guy, Kane, had the greatest life ever. On his deathbed, what's he do? He babbles a single word. Rosebud. Nobody knows what he means. Just nonsense, they think. Ravings of the imminently departing. But no. Turns out it was the name of the sled he played with and rode on when he was a kid. The sled turned out to be the final thing in his mind as he slid off into eternity."

Henny silenced the room for a few moments with his lesson in American cinema. Noah spoke first.

"But she said only numbers."

"But she wrote a bit more than numbers," Henny pointed out.

Noah banged an elderly fist onto his thigh.

"But I don't get the sense of it!" he cried. 'In anguish' might be too dramatic a description of his state, but he tended that way.

Henny carried on.

"Did she ever mention anything to you about something she missed, something she looked back on? Where did she grow up? What did she, or her father even, tell you about her life when she was a child? I'm looking for a Rosebud here."

"I never met her father, and she grew up in Philadelphia, but she…we never went back there. Not even for her father's funeral. She had…" Beamer made a hand gesture. "…brushed the place from her life."

"Why?" I asked.

"I told you. She and her father had a terrible row after she graduated from college. She wouldn't talk about it. I never knew the cause and soon learned not to pry into it, so I can't tell you very much about her childhood. She didn't like discussing it. She could be a very stubborn woman. Very. If she decided not to discuss something, it didn't get discussed. Or, in this case, after I learned my lesson, even mentioned. All I know is she went to parochial school, Catholic high school, Catholic college, had a rupture with her father, went to Margate, met me, then Brooklyn and a life together. A happy life together, except for Josh's moving to Idaho."

"What about your wife's mother?" Henny asked.

"Passed when she was seven. I got that much out of her. And as for your somewhat abrupt question about Vicky's fidelity…we worked in the store together, lived together, vacationed together… we rarely were apart, looking back. No, nothing like a dalliance was possible. Or desirable on either of our parts. No."

"So you were never apart?" Henny asked.

"No, never…well now I recall she did go back to Philadelphia once, I don't know, maybe ten years ago for a college reunion. She said she was curious about how everyone turned out."

Henny sat quiet, and I couldn't think of anything to ask. Noah got to his feet.

"Will you help me? Can you help me?"

"We'll do all we can," Henny promised.

"Thank you, thank you. Interrupt me any time of day. Here's my card. I'll write my personal cell number on the back."

Henny took Noah's card, and with both of us promising to do our best, Henny and I bid the man goodnight.

Thirteen

Henny and I traveled back to Williamsburg together after Mr. Beamer left. I knew the case had gotten to Henny because not only was he very quiet on the short subway ride, but he devoured two toothpicks to splinters on the way. Susan called me around eight to ask about Mr. Beamer but, fortunately, was on her way to some Chinatown political meeting and couldn't wait to hear my answer. Which I didn't want to give her, anyway. I'd like for once to solve a case on my own. Point, me. She did say, though, she'd stop by next day.

Henny and I went to the office on our own in the mornings, and he usually beat me in. His next morning's greeting concerned the Beamer case.

"You come up with anything last night?" he asked.

"Good morning to you, too. No. I can't imagine why Beamer's wife would repeat those numbers. Three-eight-thirteen's gotta be a date. What else could it be?"

"But it's not a date. It can't be."

"And so we call it a mystery."

Susan walked in without knocking about an hour later and apologized to me for her abrupt sign-off the previous night.

"Couldn't be helped," she explained. "Work. I gave my notice to the *World Journal* this morning. One more week."

"Not taking any time off between jobs, then?" I asked.

"If the landlord takes time off from collecting the rent and the supermarket takes time off from making me pay for food, I'll take some time off. Until then... What did your lighting neighbor want?"

There was no getting around it now, so Henny and I spilled everything we could recall about Mrs. Beamer last words. I handed Susan my copy of the notation from the datebook, and she studied it carefully.

"I can see why you thought license plate. The Pa obviously tends to that. But the one-nine-one-three-five...I know one-nine-one is the beginning of the Philadelphia zip code. So the Pa, Pennsylvania—the Philadelphia zip code. You should research the zip and see where it is. Is it where she lived as a kid?"

Henny and I looked at one another, then back at Susan. We shrugged in unison.

"Come on, boys, sharpen up. I can see where the other numbers suggest a date to you, but you're right. The thirteen is a problem—especially in a 2009 datebook. Have you thought of speaking with the son? Maybe he knows something about it. Where is he again?"

"Idaho," I answered.

"Well," Susan muttered, "can't hurt, I guess. And your lighting man is certain there's nothing that happened since they were married that bears on anything in the datebook note?"

"He says not," I responded. "He and his wife seemed to have been joined at the hip for all those years."

"If he's right," Susan said, "then it has to be something before he met her, maybe when she was growing up."

"Like Rosebud," Henny interjected.

"Like what?" Susan asked.

"Never mind him," I said. "You've given us some good ideas. We'll call the son; we'll find out more about Beamer's wife, like where she lived in Philadelphia."

Susan got to her feet.

"Keep me in the loop," she said. "Oh, which of you is going to call the son?"

"I don't know. I will," Henny offered.

"Why don't you let me do it?" Susan said. "A woman's touch. Less threatening, eh? Get the young man's number and call me. You two may want to take a trip to Philadelphia when you learn a little more. If I think of anything else, I'll let you know. And get the number for me." She left.

"I told you we should have talked to Susan," Henny said.

"Who are the detectives here, anyway? Her or us?"

"How about her and us?"

I didn't like it and frowned.

"Henny, why don't you go talk to Beamer again? Get more info about where his wife lived in Philadelphia and get the son's phone number. I'll research one-nine-one-three-five."

Our dependence on Susan's insights and abilities, I admit, had made serious inroads on my male ego. Therefore, I researched the devil out of the notation Beamer left us. When Henny returned, I waved off his report for the moment, other than to learn he'd already called and given Susan the son's phone number. I suggested I keep at my research while Henny went out to bring back some lunch. I promised I'd have my report ready by the time he got back. Henny brought back some Mexican food, a nice change, I had to admit. As we ate, we reported. Henny first.

"Susan said she'd call or stop in after she reached Josh, the son. Beamer gave me the address of Lady Beamer's childhood home." Henny flipped over a page in the small notebook he had. "Five-four-three-two Large Street. Mean anything to you?"

"Is the zip code one-nine-one-three-five?"

"I don't know."

"Hold on." I tossed my lunch debris into the metal trash can next to my desk and through the wonders of cell phone technology, I learned the Large Street address had a one-nine-one-two-four zip code. "This might be something. I noticed 19135 and 19124 are next to one another." I tapped the computer screen to indicate where I'd gotten my information.

Henny nodded but spoiled the moment by saying, "What is the something it might be?"

"We don't know yet. At least it means we don't have to go researching the entire city. If Beamer's wife's last thoughts didn't spring from her life in New York, then they had to spring from something that happened in this one-nine-one, two four-one-nine-one-three-five area. Don't you think?"

"Or college?"

"She seems never to have bothered about college after graduation."

"Except for the one reunion."

"Curiosity, Beamer said she called it. Sounds natural."

"I don't know," Henny said with a shrug. "Anything out of the norm—why the reunion—when was it?"

"He wasn't specific. Ten years ago, he said. Call him and ask."

Henny made the quick call.

"Giving it more thought, he pegged it in 2009."

"Naturally. It couldn't be March eighth, 2013. No, of course not. Why make things easy? We'll do what you said, though—look into the reunion. Something might have happened during her college years. What else?"

"Vicky's maiden name was Madison."

"Don't tell me her father's name was Oscar."

"No. Lawrence."

"Good." The idea that the universe might be sitting up there laughing at Henny and me I found annoying.

"How about you?" Henny asked. "What'd you find out?"

I'd done really sparkling research and prepared to shine.

"One-nine-one-three-five seems to be a typical, residential area, stretching from the Delaware River, the very border of Philadelphia, inland to…" I paused for a dramatic revelation. "…where the one-nine-one-two-four zip code begins."

"You already told me they abut."

Henny the buzz-kill.

"Right. Anyway, streets and houses, what you would expect, plus a big park and cemetery."

"So nothing, really, out of the ordinary. One-nine-one-two-four's similar?"

"Looked like. Anyway, the initials. NCHC. They match the National Collegiate Hockey Conference. Lots of stuff on the computer about it."

Henny gnawed his toothpick. "Do you think Vicky Madison Beamer played collegiate hockey? At a women's college? In the late sixties?"

"Uh, well, no, probably not. What about the North Central Health Care system? I found information on that. NCHC."

"It's in Philadelphia?"

"Well, no. Actually it's in Wisconsin."

Henny's head drooped. "You're killing me, Lloyd. Wisconsin?"

"We're eliminating possibilities, aren't we?" I phumphered.

"Let's eliminate running back for the Eagles, mayor of Philadelphia, and a million other things. Did you find anything helpful we might include as a possibility?"

"Why don't you go research something? See how you do."

Henny spat his gnarled toothpick into his own metal trashcan and plucked another from the box he kept in his desk drawer.

"Let's research the reunion thing. I like it as an out-of-the-norm, sore thumb sort of occurrence. She only went to one reunion, so there had to be a reason for it. Curiosity? Why curious at that specific time? What else we got happening in 2009? Check your list."

Very disgruntled, I checked the timeline I'd constructed.

"Son graduated 2006 and moved away in 2008."

"And the year of the datebook itself was 2009."

A quiet moment of thought descended on the two of us. Henny broke the silence.

"We looked the datebook over. You remember any note about a college reunion?"

I didn't and said so.

More silence reigned. An idea struck me, but after my recent research debacle, I hesitated to offer it. I considered my idea in silence for a moment, and it struck me as eminently sensible, so I offered it up.

"About the reunion you like so much." Throw a little blame on Henny, I thought, if it didn't amount to anything. "Maybe something special happened at the reunion that one year. Maybe she found out an old boyfriend was attending or…ooohh…even more startling, an old girlfriend. If you know what I mean. It was the experiment-with-everything sixties when she was at school."

"'Experiment-with-everything sixties?'"

"So I've read. Drugs, partners, music."

Henny nodded thoughtfully. "Maybe. Could be something strong enough there to haunt her on her deathbed." Henny gestured to the computer, and I went to work.

It didn't take long. The Immaculata College website had a link for the Immaculata Alumnae/Reunion office. It listed a phone number. I alerted Henny, who rolled his chair close as I punched in speakerphone.

"Immaculata Alumnae."

"Yes, hello. I'd like to get some information, please, about an old friend of mine."

"We get lots of calls like this." I heard a smile in the voice of the woman on the other end of the line. "I'll help you if I can. Some information is confidential, though. Often we take your information and pass it along to the person and let them decide what to do. You understand."

"Absolutely. The reunion of the class of 1969 which was held in 2009."

"Oh, a forty-year reunion! Yes?"

"The student's name is Vicky Beamer. Vicky Madison at the time she attended school. Beamer is her married name."

"Hold on. Let me enter…"

Henny and I waited. Forty years after graduation—a nice round number—could be a motivational time frame to look up an old love, I thought.

"Vicky Madison," came the woman's voice. "I see her name, but we don't really have much information on her. Graduated in 1969, as you said…but, no. We have no record of her ever having attended a reunion. Not one. Does she still live on Large Street? Is that her current address? No, I see we stopped sending mail to that address long ago. Do you have her current address, perhaps?"

"No," I said. "I was hoping you could help me out with it. I guess she's kind of dropped off the Earth." In a manner of speaking, she had. "Not a single reunion at all?" I repeated. Perhaps Beamer'd gotten the year wrong.

"No, we have nothing on her. There doesn't appear to be any contact with her since she graduated."

If that were true, the year Beamer provided certainly didn't matter.

"Thank you for your time." I hung up.

Henny rolled his chair back to his desk.

"This reunion thing's looking better. Beamer said she went to Philadelphia only once for a reunion. But no reunion, so she went to Philadelphia under cover of a reunion for some other reason."

"Suppose she didn't go to Philadelphia," I suggested. Henny held up a finger and phoned Beamer, who told him he remembered buying his wife's train ticket for the trip as well as her coming home with a bag of genuine Philly soft pretzels as well as a wedge of Scrapple. He thanked Beamer and hung up.

"Lloyd, I'm thinking Susan was right. We may want to make a trip to Philadelphia. We can look around. Maybe even find some people to question. How much ground can two zip codes cover?"

In what I felt to be a craven surrender, I conceded Susan's wisdom.

"Let's wait to hear from Susan before we decide," Henny advised. "See what she thinks after she talks to the kid."

I agreed and the rest of the day moved along.

Susan finally called around five o'clock, and I put her on speakerphone.

"I reached Josh, and he was surprised to hear his mother's strange fixation with those numbers at the end. He said his father hadn't mentioned it. He also said his father was very distraught the whole time he was there for the funeral, so I wouldn't put much emphasize on Mr. Beamer's not bringing it up to the boy. The real piece of emotion I took away from my conversation with the young man was both his and his mother's sadness at living thousands of miles apart. He called it his mother's grief. He remembered joking with her that he wasn't going to the moon, and they would see each other again. She really cracked up after he said that, he remembered. They even cried together. Very touching. I had tears in my eyes listening to him describe the scene. But the datebook notation meant nothing to him. I made suggestions. He thought the Pa for Pennsylvania made sense. A zip code and an inexplicable date looked right. But nothing he could put together. So, there you have it."

Henny and I quickly recounted our day for Susan. I owed Henny for omitting a report on the National Collegiate Hockey Conference and the North Central Health Care system in Wisconsin.

By conversation's end, our collective deliberations indicated a trip to Philadelphia might be worthwhile. It would take renting a car, but Henny and I did have a reasonable bank account to cover expenses. I printed out a paper to hang up on the door when we left for the day, announcing Henny and Lloyd would be away on an important investigation. I scotch taped one of our cards to it in case a new client wandered by.

A knock on the door announced Mr. Beamer.

"I brought you this," he said and handed a large book to Henny. "My wife's college yearbook from 1969. You asked about her college time, so I thought…"

We informed Mr. Beamer we were off to Philadelphia the next day, hot on the trail of his wife's final thoughts. He looked underwhelmed and unconvinced but thanked us. He returned to his store, and after I arranged for a rental car, Henny and I headed back to Williamsburg.

Fourteen

Henny and I were through the Holland Tunnel, down the Jersey Turnpike, over the Tacony Palmyra Bridge, and entered the 19135 zip code by ten-thirty next morning. Henny drove while I jotted down notes—his suggestions and mine. It didn't take long to do since there were only a couple. I read mine back to Henny.

"NCHC—the HC could be a health club or head coach," I offered.

Henny's head dropped for a moment.

"I swear you're trying to kill me, Lloyd. Could you expand on either of those?"

I couldn't.

"We scoured the woman's yearbook last night page by page," Henny correctly pointed out. "She was not on any sports team, so she had no head coach. And health club? Why not NCHC—the Nudist Camp Happiness Conglomerate?"

"Want me to look it up?" I groused. Henny chose not to respond.

"Let's go and see where she lived," Henny's suggested.

We obeyed the every command of the GPS on my phone and pulled alongside the curb in front of 5432 Large Street.

"Nothing special," Henny muttered. "I don't see any people around."

A neighborhood of two-story row houses, the backs of the houses on each block facing long driveways.

"Nobody's going to remember the Madisons," I said. "Vicky Madison left in 1969, and her father died in 1996, twenty years ago. What the hell are we looking for?" I griped in frustration.

"We're in one-nine-one-two-four now, right? They lived in one-nine-one-two-four."

"Yeah."

"Let's go back to one-nine-one-three-five and drive around. That's the number she wrote down. It has to be important. Look for something, anything. Look for those NCHC initials."

Henny pulled the car out, and we drove.

"Do you suppose they might be the initials of a person?" I asked.

"People don't usually have four initials unless they're the Duke of Bridgewater."

Henny had an answer for everything.

"Just drive," I said.

We drove down Levick Street, up Devereaux Avenue, along Bustleton Avenue, then up Frankford Avenue with a turn onto Harbison Avenue. We made this circuit twice, since those streets seemed to be the major streets of the 19135 neighborhood. Nothing struck the eye.

"No health clubs, even," Henny pointed out, a comment a little too tinged with sarcasm for my taste. "Are we going to drive these streets a third time?"

We'd turned onto Levick Street again.

"I don't know. Hey…there…there! Pull over." Henny had seen what I saw and turned onto a side street. He parked the car, and he and I walked to the police station.

"You can do the talking," Henny said.

"Get rid of the toothpick," I ordered.

Henny glared, but the toothpick went. He buttoned his gray, pin-striped double-breasted jacket, and we marched ahead.

We entered the station and walked past the 15th Precinct sign straight to the front desk, where a female officer rose from her chair and came to the counter to greet us.

"We're looking for something," I said. I took out my wallet and flashed my New York State Private Investigator's license. Colleagues, I hoped she think.

"Yes?"

"Something in the one-nine-one-three-five zip code area had meaning for someone, and all we have to go on are the initials NCHC. You're one-nine-one-three-five, right?"

"We are."

Henny explained further. "A woman died recently in New York but on her deathbed, she kept repeating certain numbers, numbers we've tracked down to this area."

"She died?" the office repeated.

"Natural causes. She was from this area originally. Grew up, went to school around here," I tossed in.

"What were the letters again?"

"NCHC."

"NCHC," the officer mumbled. "Could she have wanted to be buried near home?"

"Possible," I said. I didn't know whether it was possible or not. "Why do you ask?"

"Might be North Cedar Hill Cemetery. Only thing I can think of with those initials."

"Where's that?" Henny asked.

The officer provided directions—a five-minute drive, she claimed, and Henny and I went back to the car.

"What do you think?" Henny asked as he cranked up the engine. "Lady Beamer strike you as the sentimental sort?"

"The initials are right. It's the best we got. It's the only thing we got. Let's go see."

We drove up Frankford Avenue to Cheltenham Avenue and turned right. There lay the cemetery, a metal arch across the entryway proclaimed: NORTH CEDAR HILL CEMETERY.

Henny crept along the cemetery roadway at about 5 MPH.

"Are we looking for something?" I asked.

"The office."

"There's a building. It's got windows, so I don't think anyone's buried there."

Henny pulled into one of the six parking spots, five of which were available. As we walked toward the entrance, we had a quick discussion.

"We'll ask who got buried on March eighth, 2013," I proposed.

"We can but the datebook with the notation was from 2009."

"This whole thing is way out of order."

"We can try the only two names we know."

"Vicky, her father, and her husband...widower. That's three."

"Her husband's still above ground. I don't think he's connected with the cemetery, do you?" Again the faint smell of sarcasm filled the car.

"No, I guess not."

The conversation ended as Henny opened the office door, and a man with an extraordinarily long face, wearing a solemn black suit, white shirt, thin black tie, and standing about six-foot-four got up from behind a desk. With a face full of professional gloom, he welcomed us.

"Please, sit. I'm sorry for your loss."

"No, no," I corrected him. "We didn't lose anything…I mean anybody."

Henny produced his P.I. license, and the funereal funeral man's face got even longer.

Henny told as much of the tale as he thought necessary. He concluded with, "Can you give us any information about a Vicky Madison or Vicky Beamer?"

"Or even a Lawrence Madison," I added. "They're the only names we have."

The Addams Family sibling got onto his computer.

"No Vicky Madison or Vicky Beamer in our records," he reported, which amounted to exactly no help to us. "Wait. Did you say Lawrence Madison?"

"Yes," Henny responded.

"We have a Lawrence Madison buried here."

"Died in 1996?" I asked.

"Why, yes, that is the year."

"What do you think, Henny? Take a look?" I asked.

"Might as well. We're here. How can we find it?" he asked.

"I'll write the location down for you." He snapped off a post-it. "Section three; Rows eight by thirteen."

Henny took the post-it, and he and I froze. He checked what the merchant of doom had written.

"Three-eight-thirteen," he said to me, and my stomach did a little dance.

"Thank you," we both sputtered and sped out on our treasure hunt. We found area 3 and walked along the outskirts of even numbered markers. When we reach eight, Henny sent me to the corner of the expansive plot. I found the odd number markers going in the other direction and walked to 13. Henny strode one way, and I went the other until we met. A brief perusal of the tombstones gave us LAWRENCE MADISON; August 1, 1912—February 5, 1996. BELOVED FATHER OF VICTORIA. A dozen roses which looked about halfway through their life span sat in a vase permanently affixed in the ground before the tombstone.

I read the grave marker three times.

"Something funny," Henny muttered. "Beloved by whom? Couldn't be Victoria. Noah said they didn't get along big time."

"Who puts these flowers here?" I wondered.

"Let's go ask."

We headed back to the office to confront the avatar of mortality. His computer revealed a flower delivery every two weeks by the Floralists, a place with a business arrangement with North Cedar Hill, located two blocks down Frankford Avenue. Henny and I were off on the scent.

The flowers, it turned out, had been coming since mid-2009, and deliveries were paid through December 2018.

"Who put the order through?" Henny asked.

"Let me see. It originated in Brooklyn. Ms. Victoria Beamer."

"Then I suggested we go back to the cemetery office." I sat contentedly behind my desk later that evening, explaining to Susan how Henny and I cracked the case, making certain she realized this final nugget of information originated from an idea in my brain. Henny sat quietly at his desk, jacket buttoned, gnawing on toothpicks, one after the other. If he'd taken up cigarettes, 1940s' style, the way he'd taken up toothpicks, he'd've been coughing up blood into a handkerchief by this time. His fingers, only two of them, drummed nervously on his desktop.

"What did the scary man tell you?" Susan asked.

Apparently, I'd exaggerated the dire appearance of the cemetery chief.

"The headstone. I asked whether it was original or whether it had been replaced since 1996. He confirmed the headstone had been replaced—delivered the summer of 2009. You can guess who supplied it."

"Wow! She came to really miss her daddy."

"She did! Oh, he's here."

We'd phoned Mr. Beamer when we got back from Philadelphia and asked him to come over to our office when he'd shut up shop for the day.

"Are there more things you want to ask me?" Beamer said.

Susan got up and offered Mr. Beamer our client chair. She stood off to the side, reporter's notebook in hand.

I checked with Henny, and he merely swung his two drumming fingers in my direction. I should handle the explanation.

"We know what your wife meant with her note in the datebook and with her last words," I said.

Mr. Beamer grabbed the chair arms for support and half rose. He plopped back down and said, "Is it true? How did you…? What was she saying?"

"Henny and I and Susan…have you met Susan?" Mr. Beamer acknowledged Susan. "We've talked over what we learned, and we think we have the picture clear."

"Not something bad. Please tell me it's not something hurtful."

"Nothing bad, nothing hurtful, I assure you. When your son left for good in 2008, your wife was very upset, true?"

"Oh, she was heartbroken, inconsolable."

"We're assuming the loss of her child, so to speak, put her in mind of her own father and how he'd lost his child— herself—forty years earlier. She never saw her father again, or more to the point perhaps—he never saw her again. Do you know the word empathy, Mr. Beamer?"

"Empathy? Is it like sympathy?"

"Yes. Feeling the sorrow and pain another person feels and identifying with the person. Your wife felt, we believe, a growing empathy for her father. She knew what it meant, what it felt like, to have a child disappear out of your life. We don't know the cause of the original rupture between father and daughter, but it doesn't matter. She knew the pain she'd caused her father because of the parting with her own son, though amicable in her case. And she no doubt felt her own pain over the split with her father. She never went to the college reunion she told you about in 2009."

"She lied to me!"

"With good reason. Motivated by her own son's leaving, we believe she went to Philadelphia to visit her father's grave. It would be the only time in her life she would visit. She bought a new headstone for the grave. The stone read: BELOVED FATHER OF VICTORIA."

"Oh my god," Beamer muttered. "And she composed that?"

"Yes, plus she arranged for flowers to be placed on the grave every two weeks. That will stop soon—the end of this year. Three-eight-thirteen is the cemetery's official code for the location of the grave. One-nine-one-three-five is the zip code of the cemetery. NCHC stood for North Cedar Hill Cemetery. Pa was Pennsylvania. All of those letters and numbers were needed to set up the delivery with the flower store and perhaps the delivery of the headstone. She placed the order for flowers in Brooklyn, and it's filled by a florist two blocks from the cemetery."

Susan added, "Your wife was thinking of her father as she lay dying, Mr. Beamer. Regretting what had passed between them."

No one spoke. I noticed Henny's two fingers speed up their tattooing of the desktop. He leaned his head back and sniffed.

"My poor darling," Mr. Beamer said softly. "To miss her father so much and never mention." He gave me a wan smile. "She was always very proud, very stubborn."

"That's the story, Mr. Beamer," I concluded.

"Those flowers. Can I continue to have them delivered to the grave?"

Henny gave another sniff and turned his face away.

"I'm sure you can. I'll give you the necessary info tomorrow."

He thanked me and rose.

"I'll come back tomorrow morning to pay you for your services," Mr. Beamer said. "I need to go home now."

"Sure," I said.

"No," said Henny. "We were glad to help you out. This one's on us."

I gaped but quickly got myself under control.

"Tomorrow, I will be in," Mr. Beamer repeated and left the office.

Henny gave a sniff so prodigious I expected to see the paper clips lying on his desk take flight and disappear up his nose.

"Are you crying?" I asked.

He spun and offered me the back of his chair.

"No," he answered. "Allergies. Bad time of year."

Susan and I looked at one another and shrugged. Some tough guy, I thought.

"I'll leave you two alone," Susan said. "Talk to you soon," she promised and departed.

I swear I saw the back of Henny's shoulders going up and down. Since I hadn't the faintest idea of what to do with a snuffling detective, I didn't do anything. When, finally, Henny eased his chair back to normal, I said, "We did pretty good on this case. Solved it ourselves."

"Yeah, I guess we're getting better."

"Maybe we should celebrate with a little Boone's That's All?"

Henny gave himself a shake and a stentorian throat clearing.

"Damn, yes we should. We are getting better."

"It's in your bottom drawer, pal."

Henny got out the bottle and paper cups and poured.

I raised my cup. "To our greatest, and for the most part, first unaided success."

"And to Victoria and Lawrence Madison. One thing. I don't think the Pa in the notation meant Pennsylvania. I think it meant 'father.' You know—ma and pa?"

I swear I saw Henny's lower lip quiver, but he managed to sip his drink deftly, notwithstanding.

After one drink. Henny muttered the syllable "pa" and insisted on a short, second drink. I concurred. I thought he needed it.

Fifteen

The Corpse in the Doorway

Some time passed, and our bank accounts dwindled, but on a Tuesday in November, one of Henny's fondest wishes came true. We sat at our desks, Henny reading *The Maltese Falcon* for what he swore was the eighth time, me wondering why Susan hadn't called. We'd seen each other at least once a week, and I'd phoned her each day since I'd seen her last, so I knew I'd held up my end of things.

You could sometimes fry eggs on the radiators in our office, so I'd cracked open one of the windows to relieve the desert atmosphere. Henny and I both heard them—two quick pops.

"Couldn't be," I chuckled. I don't particularly like the word 'chuckled.' Henny would say it certainly wasn't a word in the *noir* vocabulary. But, to be scrupulously accurate, I did chuckle. Henny went back to his book, and I returned to my stubborn cocoon of refusing to call Susan more than once a day. Soon, two dolorous knocks caused our heads to swivel toward our door. Henny tossed his book down and hurried to answer. He opened the door and a woman, perhaps thirty or thirty-five years old, took two steps inside the office, dropped to her knees, and stared blankly at Henny before falling forward. From the noise her head made connecting…bonk!…with our wooden floor, I knew the worst had happened.

I rushed over and knelt across from Henny, who had his thumb pressed against the woman's neck.

"I don't feel a pulse," he said. "Ohhh!" Henny pointed to two small holes in the back of the woman's heavy blue coat.

"Shot! Turn her over."

We did. There were no holes in the front, so I bent as close to her nose as possible but detected nothing going in or coming out. I, too, tested the artery in her neck. Nothing. I tried the other side of her neck. Nothing going on there either. She appeared dead on both sides.

"We better get nine-one-one," I said.

"I'll call," Henny said. "You look through her stuff. The cops get here, they'll take everything away. Write everything down."

As Henny made the call, I frisked the woman. She carried no handbag, so I went through the two pockets of her coat. In one pocket I found a small wallet and some keys. She wore slacks and a thin, light pink sweater. The slacks had two empty pockets, except for a short stub of chalk. I went back to my desk and looked through the wallet. I ignored the twenty-something in bills and copied down the information from her driver's license, as well as a NYSUT/UFT—teachers' unions—membership card. The name on the two credit cards matched the name on the license and membership card. I put everything back into the wallet and the wallet and keys back into the coat pocket. I rolled her over the way she fell.

"Ambulance on the way," Henny said. "What'd you find?"

"Her name is Alania Simpson. She lives in Queens and appears to be a teacher."

"Why teacher?"

"Union membership card. This chunk of chalk from her pocket."

"That all?"

"Two credit cards, keys, and a little money."

We heard a siren. I went to the windows and a minute later saw an ambulance pull up outside.

"You tell them the third floor?"

"Yeah."

"Want to meet them at the elevator? No, I'll go."

Moments later, two men and a woman wheeled a gurney into our office, but it went unused. They fussed over the body, shocked it a few times and made it jump, but could only pronounce the woman beyond earthly help. They looked the woman over.

"This woman's been shot," the female medic announced. "You know what happened?"

Henny answered. "Nope. She knocked at our door; I opened it, she took two steps inside and plop."

"You know who she is?"

"Never saw her before."

Henny was pretty good at lying while answering a question accurately. Reasonably accurately.

"You call the cops?" one of the males asked.

"We called you," Henny responded. "We didn't know she'd been shot."

One male paramedic looked at the other. "Well, we'll have to leave her where she is until the cops get here. They'll want to look things over and ask you guys some questions. You want to get them, Charlie?"

Charlie stepped outside, and three minutes later two police officers made the rattling trip up our elevator. They looked at the body, seemingly unaffected by the tragedy. Henny, though, had already chewed his way through his sixth toothpick.

One police officer, Officer Ong his nameplate read, said, "Gotta leave things as they are till forensics gets here. You two better stay around. Any problem with that?"

"Nope," I said. "We work here." Henny and I went back to our chairs. The cops and the paramedics chatted until, half an hour later, our office became a busy crime scene. Henny and I watched the goings on carefully. It seemed odd to me, witnessing something happening live I'd seen numerous times on TV. Maybe forty minutes after the crew arrived, the paramedics carted the body off, and things returned to normal. While the crime scene crew did their inspection, two detectives, who'd arrived minutes after them, asked Henny and me for everything we knew. It took about a minute to satisfy them.

"We'll be in touch if we need you," one of the two said. The harshness of his voice nearly induced me to offer a salute—me a private, him a general, but I stifled the impulse. The door closed, and Henny turned to me.

"We have one! Our first murder case!"

I don't wish anyone to think Henny a blood-thirsty, morbid fellow, but to Henny, a detective working on a murder case achieved the same lofty level of prominence as a ball player making it to the All Star Game.

"We don't have much to work with," I pointed out. "Also, nobody's hired us to do anything."

"The dead lady came to see us. She had to have a reason."

"We don't know that. Maybe we were the nearest refuge. She'd just been shot, you know. We heard the two shots."

"You don't look for refuge on the third floor with two bullets in you," Henny argued.

"No, I guess not. You make a good point."

"With her life's last blood, she staggered to us, to me and you. We were her destination. I know it. Why?"

The phone rang, and we were about to find out why.

I picked up. "Henny and Lloyd Detective Agency."

"Oh, good. It's you. Is Alania still there? Alania Simpson?"

I bugged my eyes at Henny.

"No," I answered. "Who's this?" I covered the mouthpiece and whispered. "Someone looking for the dead woman." I hit speakerphone as Henny rolled his chair nearer.

"Gloria Wilcox. How long ago did she leave your office? I'm covering her class, and she's late already. The AP's breathing down my neck."

I heard a voice in the background shouting, "Where's the stinking teacher?" followed by the lady on the phone saying, "Be quiet, Victor." I looked to Henny for guidance. He gave a shrug and whispered, "You might as well tell her."

I drew in a deep breath and did what needed to be done.

"I'm afraid your friend won't be coming back."

"What! What do you mean she won't be back? I have another class coming in."

"I'm afraid Ms. Simpson has met with an accident, a serious accident."

"An accident? Is she all right. Has she been taken to a hospital?"

"I'm afraid she's dead."

A piercing scream wrapped around an agonized "What?" exploded from our phone speaker. "No, no, no. What do you mean? That can't be!"

"I'm afraid it's true. Ms. Simpson died in our office the moment she arrived. She'd been shot."

"Shot! That's impossible! They would never do such a thing."

Henny perked up, and so did I.

"Tell her we'll meet her," Henny whispered. "We'll go to her."

"My associate and I will come and see you and explain everything, if you'd like."

"Shot! I don't believe it. I don't believe it. My God."

A moment of silence ensued; then I tried again.

"Should we come to your school?" I asked.

"No, no. Not here. Please, not here."

"Where are you? Where's your school?"

"Chinatown."

I thought quickly. "I can send a man to pick you up. Our office is nearby. He'll bring you here."

"Yes, yes. That'd be better."

"Look for a well-dressed younger man standing in front of your school. He'll be wearing a gray fedora with a small, blue feather. He'll bring you here in a cab."

"Yes, yes. My god, I have to tell the AP. What a nightmare! Okay, three o'clock… Forty Division Street, on the sidewalk in front of the main entrance."

"He'll be there." I signed off.

Gloria Wilcox must certainly have bustled out the door after work. Henny had her back in our office by three fifteen. Sniffling and handkerchief in hand, she took our client chair.

"Did you tell Ms. Wilcox the details?" I asked Henny.

Henny shook his head.

"It was my fault. I tried to explain to your partner…" Gloria began tearfully.

"Ms. Wilcox was too upset listen to any explanation," Henny said. He gave me a surreptitious eye roll to indicate the extent of the ravings he'd been subjected to in the taxi.

"I'm calm. Now," said Gloria. "Please. What happened?"

I gave a brief account of the briefer encounter.

"Shot! Shot! Oh, this is too awful. Unbelievable. Did she say anything? Do you know who did this?"

Henny said, "I opened the door. She took two steps and collapsed. Didn't say a word."

Gloria's hand went to her forehead, her elbow supported by the chair arm—a gesture of finality. It had sunk in.

Softly, I went on. "You said something about 'they would never do such a thing.' Can you tell us who you meant?"

Gloria shook her head. "No, it couldn't be. Forget what I said. I was upset, rambling."

Henny and I shared a look. Neither of us believed her.

"Do you know why your friend came to see us?" Henny asked. "We might still be able to help out if we knew why she did."

Gloria stared hard at Henny, then at me. A decision pended.

"Someone did this awful thing to her," Henny said. "You can't let it stand."

Gloria softly sobbed. Henny'd gotten to her. We gave her time. Then she began.

"I'm an artist. I paint. Oils. I make silk screens, prints. I couldn't find a gallery which would show my work, though."

More sobbing.

"Would you like some coffee?" I asked. I don't believe I mentioned the coffee maker, but we had one, along with a tiny refrigerator. Henny insisted we needed a few amenities.

"No, no. Thanks. Alania found a gallery, the Ripov Gallery in Chelsea. They would show work they approved of, but for a fee. They rented wall space, in other words. Alania always encouraged me. She liked what I produced. I told her I didn't think it wise to be throwing my money away. I'm a teacher, not a hedge fund manager. But she wouldn't take no for an answer. She offered to put up half the fee for a half share of the sale of anything I hung up on my rented wall space. That sounded fair—more than fair. It came to about twenty-five hundred dollars each. Not cheap to get an opening night and a month's worth of public and internet exposure.

"Somehow, someone saw my work and two weeks into the show bought a silk screen—the Twin Towers. A few weeks later, the gallery asked whether I could produce ten more silk screens of the Twin Towers for the purchaser of the first copy, and they offered to put other of my works on their website at no charge. Alania and I made our money back plus a nice bonus over the month. When the show ended, the gallery offered me free space for three months for two of my silk screens of their choosing. I thought this was wonderful. Alania and I celebrated and she…she…"

A severe bout of sobbing halted the story. Henny and I patiently waited.

"She said she'd made her money and refused any further income from my work. I would have offered her—I did offer her—ten per cent from the work I sold off the free space, but she absolutely refused." After a brief pause, Gloria looked from Henny to me and said, "She was a true friend."

I certainly agreed with her but stayed mum.

"What went wrong?" Henny asked.

"Alania stopped me in the school hallway one morning, very upset. She said she'd googled me the night before and found one of my Twin Towers silk screens for sale at a gallery in Amsterdam priced at twelve thousand dollars. Ripov Gallery sold them for fifteen hundred."

"Quite a mark-up," Henny said.

"The month after my show closed, five of the silk screens I hung in the free wall space they'd given me sold. I presume to the same person. The gallery wouldn't say. They don't want their artists selling behind their back. Fifteen hundred dollars each. I finally felt like a success. Until Alania found one of those five for sale at a Berlin gallery for thirteen thousand dollars. She was certain I was getting ripped off. I told her whoever bought my silk screens could resell them for whatever amount he or she wanted. She asked me to suppose they weren't being resold but were simply being sold—by my home gallery, for fifteen thousand or so. They gave me half of the fifteen hundred they told me they sold it for, and they kept the rest. Imagine that, she said.

"Alania called the gallery and demanded an explanation. I listened to her call. She threatened to expose them if she found out they were selling my work on the sly. She demanded to know the name of the person who bought the works from the gallery. They wouldn't say. She promised to find the buyer nonetheless and determine the truth. The gallery owner got on his high horse and, my god, you never heard such yelling and screaming from Alania. She could really go off when she wanted. She actually visited the gallery people. I don't know where she got the nerve or why she was so dedicated to my cause."

Another sobbing break.

"Finally, she told them she'd hire private detectives to investigate, and they wouldn't know whether they were selling art to a genuine buyer or someone who would turn them in and rip the scab off their scheme."

"Rip the scab," Henny repeated, his eyes shining in admiration at the *noir* turn of phrase.

"I was naturally upset at possibly being robbed, so to speak, but I told Alania she'd done enough already. It was my job to see to my interests. But she kept on. She called the gallery one last time, got no helpful information, and told them she was going straight to a private detective agency she knew of. She found your names online, and you were the nearest to the school. Today, I covered her class after lunch so she had enough time to come to your office and get back to school. I'm an art teacher."

"Why didn't you go to the police?" I asked.

"Alania didn't think we had enough real evidence, and the police are busy with so many things. She thought threatening to hire private eyes would frighten the gallery more than saying we planned to report them to the police. I heard her scream into the phone that police had to follow the law, but private eyes could investigate anyway they wanted."

Gloria didn't sob but did pause to regroup.

"At last Alania told them if she or I didn't hear something back from the gallery that very day, she would seek professional help tomorrow. That tomorrow was today."

More sobbing. Back under control, Gloria asked, "Was she right? Was Alania right? Can you investigate better than the police?"

Depending on circumstances, I knew Henny and I would be more adept at tracking down things the police weren't much interested in. I offered a measured response.

"Sometimes."

"I better go to the police on my own, don't you think? They need to know why she came here. Of course, I should."

"Yes, you should," Henny agreed. "But if you'd like us to look into the situation on our own, we're available."

"I would. Oh, yes, please. I have some money to pay you from the art work I've sold."

I half expected soft-hearted, hard-boiled Henny to give another 'this one's on us." Thankfully, he didn't. Yet. I'd talk to him about it.

"You can count on us," Henny said. "We'll need all the information you can give us, though."

Henny and I got out our pads and pens and took down everything Gloria could think to tell us.

Sixteen

Naturally, I called Susan and put her wise to what had gone on in our office. The next day in the *Post*, and under her very first byline, she outlined the basic details of the murder. She mentioned Henny's and my name, this time including 'Detective Agency.' I wasn't sure being known as a crime scene would drum up much business, but who can predict the vagaries of the human mind? Susan kept back the side details about the art scam since, as yet, the art scam existed only as a possibility.

Henny beat me in to the office that morning, as usual. I'd taken the stairs when I didn't see the elevator waiting for me, and when I stepped inside our door, there stood Henny, making mouths into the good-sized, round mirror we'd hung on one wall. As I watched, he jostled his eyebrows up and down, slowly, then quickly. He balled up his hands, opened them, gave what looked like a karate chop to the right, all while shimmying his shoulders. I feared the poor boy had been into the Boone's That's All.

"What the hell are you doing?" I asked.

My question brought Henny's shenanigans to a halt.

"It can't be done," he said. "I don't see it. It's not possible."

"Care to explain?" I asked. I took my seat and spun my chair his way.

Henny walked to his desk and picked up *The Maltese Falcon*. "Here, read this. Tell me what you think."

He handed me the book and pointed to a line and a quarter he'd highlighted. I read, "He made angry gestures with mouth, eyebrows, hands, and shoulders."

"So?"

"So? That's Hammett describing Sam Spade. Go. You do it. Go the mirror. How do you make angry gestures with your 'mouth, eyebrows, hands, and shoulders?' It can't be done. Do it. Do it. I dare you."

"Shoulders is definitely a stretch," I agreed.

"And all at the same time! He must have looked like a string puppet in a hurricane. I'll never understand that line in a million years. It aggravates me every time I read it." Henny snatched the book back from me and dropped it onto his desk. "Did you see today's *Post*? Susan did us right." I held up the day's paper and said I had.

"Gloria Wilcox already called," Henny reported, falling into his chair, clearly disappointed over not being able to make his mouth, eyebrows, hands, and shoulders work in sync to show Spade-level anger.

"What'd she say?"

"She went to the police right from here yesterday and told them everything she told us."

"Their response?"

"They told her they'd be in touch. She wasn't impressed."

"What do you think we ought to do?"

Our office door opened unceremoniously, and a detective I recognized from the day before entered.

Henny reached for a toothpick and said, "Come in."

"I'm already in. You two the ones Gloria Wilcox told me about?"

"We are," Henny answered, toothpick twirling a mile a minute.

"Why didn't you mention her when we were here yesterday?"

"Didn't know about her." I had no qualms about letting Henny handle the conversation. "She called us after you left. You talked to her. You know that."

Henny's comment silenced the detective but brought a scowl to his face.

"You got a name?" Henny asked.

"Yeah. My mother provided me with every luxury at birth."

"Want to share it with us?"

"Detective Thursday to you."

Henny perked up. "Thursby? First name's not Floyd, is it?"

"Thursday. Thursday. Like the day of the week."

Henny settled back down. "Oh. So you were born on a Thursday, eh?"

"No, a Tuesday."

"Your mother must have been confused."

"My last name's Thursday, not my first. My mother didn't have anything to do with that, did she? And leave my mother out of this. Look, the police will handle this murder. Don't get in our way, one. Two, you stumble across something might help us, you let me know." Detective Thursday tossed a business card on Henny's desk. "I want to know everything you know the minute you know it. Got it?"

"Don't crowd us…"

If Henny's next word had been "flatfoot," I think I'd have gone through one of our two windows and hoped for the best. But it wasn't.

"…Detective. We got a job to do, too. A living to earn. Let's deal. Here, take my card. You find out something good, share with us. We'll do the same for you."

"You'll do for me 'cause I'm telling you to. Or else."

Henny and the detective locked eyes, and I wondered at Henny's audacity.

"Don't forget," Detective Thursday ordered. He spun on his heel and made his exit, leaving the office door wide open. Henny went to close the door and paused, his hand on the knob, his eyes riveted on Thursday, who stood glaring back as he waited for the elevator, which I heard clanking his way. Henny gave the door a subtle push and went back behind his desk.

"Was that great?" he cried.

"What were you doing? Wait, don't tell me. Your Sam Spade impersonation?"

"Exactly! How was I? Now we have an in with a newspaper reporter on a great metropolitan newspaper and a hard-nose detective to deal with. Oh, man. Life is great!"

I let Henny bask in his fantasy-become-reality moment. I saw his lips moving and guessed he was replaying the whole conversation back to himself. I turned my mind to the case and the question we'd left unanswered. What exactly should we do? The art gallery seemed an obvious place—the only place—to start. I cranked up the computer and found the Ripov Gallery website. I jotted down the address on West Twenty-Fifth Street. The phrase "Art chosen by our own curator" caught my eye, and my detective antennae waggled and buzzed at the word 'curator.' Very fancy terminology for a gallery renting out its wall space. I easily imagined the curator, so called, leafing through the portfolios of desperate artists, popping bon bons into his/her mouth while picking the lucky ones and sending off the good news to the artist, along with a heavy emphasis on where to send the check.

I clicked on the gallery's submission link and read the come-on. The gallery promised a gala opening night, one hundred postcards (postage not inc.) for the artist, a press release (I don't recall ever seeing one in all the years I'd been reading newspapers), and a fifty-percent share of any sales. It struck me as a business Henny and I could have run successfully and gotten a lot richer a lot quicker than we were doing at present. But we were born detectives, and we both knew it.

I interrupted Henny's time travel journey to his recent past.

"Henny, the gallery has an opening tonight. I think we should go. Get the lay of the land. See what things looked like to Gloria Wilcox and Alania Simpson when they got roped in."

Henny's nostalgia-induced smiled faded, and he rejoined me back on our home planet.

"Yes, good idea. Susan, too." He quickly held up a hand as if he were Diana Ross—"Stop, In the Name of Love."

"Don't start on we don't need her or want her. Reporters are valuable to us, same as hard-nose detectives."

"I think the proper term is 'hard-nosed'."

"Whatever. As long as his nose is hard, I'm satisfied. What time's the opening?"

"Six. I'll tell Susan to meet us there at six-fifteen. Good enough for you?"

"Fine. I'll walk over to Wilcox's school at three and see if she's got anything more to say about things. Heh! Did you hear me tell Thursday, 'Don't crowd me, copper?'"

I'd heard him say seventy-five percent of that sentence, but decided to let Henny be Henny and not rain on his parade. I phoned Susan, and set up the evening.

Henny left the office at two thirty. When he returned at about a quarter to five, he carried a shopping bag in each hand.

"Wilcox have anything new to offer?" I asked. Henny put the two bags on his desk.

"No, nothing we didn't already know."

"You tell her we were going to the opening tonight?"

"Yeah."

"And?"

Henny took a moment.

"Yes, and…" I urged.

"She said to be careful and pointed out these people were killers…if her version of things is the right version."

"She makes a good point."

"Got me thinking. Her friend's killer plugged her friend right in front of our building, maybe even in the building. He might have had us staked out and seen you and me come in that day…or leave that night. He might know what we look like."

Henny'd succeeded in considerably diminishing my enthusiasm for going to the opening, now an hour away.

"I stopped in a store on Broadway and got us these."

Henny pulled hairpieces, wigs, two fake scars, a feathery boa, and god knows what else out of the two shopping bags.

"We go in disguise," he said in a ta-da tone of voice.

I had no words. Henny tossed me one of the hairpieces.

"You like this one?"

"Yeah, this'd be great if I wanted to look like Harpo Marx or Little Orphan Annie. You must be nuts."

"It was on sale. Here, how about this one?"

He tossed me something recognizably belonging to the human species. In fact, I kind of liked it. Brown hair, loosely flowing to the collar. It had some artistic panache to it, quite appropriate for our evening's adventure. Intrigued, I walked over to the desk and chose a matching mustache. I forwent the boa or any scarring, other than to my dignity, perhaps. When I'd put myself together, Henny complimented me.

"Nice! Go take a look."

I checked myself out in the mirror. Whoa! Definitely a new me.

Henny geared up in a pompadoured blond hairpiece with matching blond mustache. I started to point out that his black eyebrows didn't match, but I checked myself. It was getting late, and we had to get moving. Henny, though, had still another ruse or two up his sleeve.

"Look," he said, "if the murderer saw us come or go, he'll recognize our coats." We'd both worn light tan, knee-length coats—1940s' style with the wide lapels and big cloth belt around the middle—to work. "We can't use them tonight. Here."

From his shopping bag, Henny pulled out two white sweatshirts emblazoned with a large red apple and NYC stitched across the apple.

"We put these under our shirts to keep warm and go with our suit jackets, no topcoats. Two sweatshirts for five bucks!"

Henny's last touch was a new fedora, plain, black, and featherless.

"Five bucks," he pointed out. "I gotta remember where I got it. They had about a hundred of them." Henny had disguised us and saved money at the same time.

"You wrapping yourself in the boa?" I asked.

"Bah. The counter guy threw it in for free. Funny man."

We tinkered with our new personas, then grabbed a taxi and headed uptown.

The Ripov Gallery filled the second floor of a building situated halfway between Tenth and Eleventh Avenues on the downtown side of the street. Henny and I awaited our turn in the tiny elevator lobby and took the second trip up. The gallery formed a large H. The empty space under the cross passage was the entrance aisle from the elevator. The cross was a counter lined with half-filled plastic cups of white wine. A door behind the counter led to the space beyond the cross. Temporary walls divided the two long, wide arms of the H, the walls angling every which way, creating acres of wall space. I could see how this gallery-renting-wall-space business would be lucrative even if a single painting never got sold. Milling art lovers flowed slowly from wall to wall, artist to artist.

"You ever been to one of these?" Henny asked.

"Nope."

"Nobody's forking over any loot for the wine. Must be on the house."

Henny put his theory to the test and walked up the counter. He smiled graciously at the two young women who busily poured wine to replace the plastic cups carried away by grateful patrons. Henny took two cups and returned to me. As he left the counter, one of the young women made a "what-was-that" face to the other. I knew what she meant. Henny's dark eyebrows contrasted glaringly with his fake blond pompadour and fake blond mustache. They looked like a couple pieces of licorice separating a sun-kissed ocean wave and a caterpillar. So much for not drawing attention to ourselves. I promised myself I'd be the wine runner for the rest of the evening.

"See Susan anywhere?" I asked, taking a cup of wine.

"Man, you could play a great game of hide-and-seek in this place. Nooks and crannies everywhere. Let's go peek behind all the walls."

We found Susan standing in front of the two silk screens Gloria Wilcox left behind. They were tucked in a corner on one of the real walls of the building. The printed note beneath indicated a $1500 price tag for each and included a short biography of Gloria Wilcox, artist/teacher.

"Hi," said Susan offering us a bright smile and a toast with her plastic cup. "I see you found the free wine. Are we going to a long-running Halloween party from here?"

Henny explained his rationale for the disguises.

"Anyway, here they are," Susan said. "They're nice."

The Twin Towers silk screen Gloria'd mentioned was done all in different shades of blue. Very spare lines, no frills. I liked it. The other offered a more traditional bowl of fruit in its natural colors. Nice, too, but the Twin Towers piece had a much more haunting quality to it, as I'm sure you can imagine.

"What do you think we should be looking for?" Susan asked.

"Wander around," came a thick Irish brogue from over my shoulder. "We have so many beautiful pieces in this show."

We were addressed by a large man with curly blond hair, dressed in a plaid kilt. He wore what looked like elf shoes and carried what I took to be a six-foot-long walking stick...or a monstrous shillelagh, considering his costume. A semi-military riband pinned with three semi-military medals slashed diagonally across his chest. He patted my shoulder and moved on.

"What was that?" Henny asked.

"He's the gallery owner," Susan answered. "His outfit was the first thing I noticed when I got here, so I asked. Whitney Amster's his name."

"Whitney Amster," Henny repeated. "That's some damn name, but he's somebody we'll need to talk to."

"Let's look at the art for a while," Susan suggested, and we took a slow boat tour of the nooks and crannies of the maximized wall space. When we crossed from one arm of the H to the other, we each grabbed a new cup of wine, and I grabbed a sheaf of stapled papers listing the name of each artist along with the titles of the artist's pieces and the price for each. There were sixteen artists listed. If I remembered correctly, it cost Gloria Wilcox some five thousand bucks to display her work. Sixteen artists times five thousand came to eighty thousand dollars. And the show changed every month, so times twelve. Nearly a million dollars. Plus any sales. Sheesh.

I kept my eye on Amster as he swaggered around his gallery, jovial, welcoming, chatting people up. Easy enough to do on a million bucks a year.

"We can't talk to him in the middle of all of this," I pointed out. "Too crowded and noisy, plus he's keeping himself occupied."

Susan held up one hand to Henny and me and walked off to say something to Amster. She flashed her press card and smiled like a beauty queen. Amster beamed a full, hundred-watt smile back at her. Susan rejoined us.

"Let's go have something to eat. Bocca di Bacco's nearby. He agreed to an interview when the opening ended. Eight, a little after."

We walked the six blocks to the restaurant where we'd nabbed Prudence Holiman and David Toledo and had something at the bar—Henny got his mushroom bruschetta again—limiting ourselves to one additional drink on top of the cheap gallery wine, and by eight, we were back at the gallery, waiting for it to clear out.

The last person went through the doors at eight-fifteen, cup of wine in hand. Amster locked the door behind the man and bustled our way, radiating the largest smile the world has ever known.

"This is very exciting," Amster said, directing us behind the counter through a door and into a well-appointed, though windowless, office. His brogue rolled over us in great, green waves. He pulled some superior red wine from a cabinet—Kendall-Jackson, the label promised—and poured it into genuine wineglasses. A fellow of considerable charm stood before us. "A major newspaper interested in our gallery. Very exciting indeed." Three of us sat on a lovely red sofa while Amster angled a plush blue chair for himself. A diminutive woman appeared through a doorway directly to Amster's right. If she stood five feet tall, that would be a stretch. Or better put, if she stretched, the top of her head might hit the five-foot mark. She appeared to be in Amster's age range and was very well put together. A number of places and things on the woman jiggled as she walked past us on her very high high-heels.

"Mildred, these people are interviewing us for the *New York Post*," Amster reported to her. The woman smiled at us and threw Amster a kiss.

"My darling wife. And the gallery curator," he said. "Now, what can I do for you?"

Not for the first time did I appreciate having Susan along. Even Henny deferred to her. At first.

"You have some exquisite pieces on display," Susan began. I vowed to remember the word "exquisite" for the next time I wanted to schmooze somebody. "Is the work you choose always of such a high caliber?"

Amster babbled on about the wonders of his contribution to the New York art scene and how he gave opportunity to deserving artists other galleries had no time for. He left out the part about their paying for the exposure.

Susan threw in a few questions to keep him going, and after fifteen minutes or so said, "There is one thing I'd like to clear up."

"Yes?"

"Rumors are rife about certain galleries taking advantage of their artists and selling their work for much more than is listed and not sharing the profit with the artist— say, selling pieces in Europe where the artist is unlikely to hear about it. Have you heard those rumors?"

I saw Henny tilt his head back, preparing for the blizzard of denials I also expected. Didn't happen.

"I have. I have. I've been accused of doing such a thing."

Mildred came bustling back into the room on her way to the inner office.

"Mildred, darling, I've mentioned to you the phone calls I've received and the woman who came here complaining about our works being resold at high prices in the Netherlands. It appears to be happening throughout the Chelsea galleries." Amster gestured to Susan as if she should pick up the story from there.

"I really can't say how widespread it is," Susan cautioned. "I was hoping to find out from you."

Mildred patted Amster on the top of his bushy head and disappeared behind the closed door of her office.

"Wonderful woman," Amster said proudly. "Couldn't do without her. No, I really have not heard about it happening other than from the woman I mentioned representing an artist who claims I'm selling her work overseas for much more than I report to the artist. I can only tell you what I told her. Anyone can resell anything they buy from us at whatever price they choose to set. I have no control over that, especially if it's happening thousands of miles away. I can't see how that would be a widespread phenomenon, though. There is so much art competing with itself. It might happen, resales for large amounts, but it would be a lightning bolt strike of good luck for someone, and probably not the artist. Although, the artist I refer to…"

Henny made his presence known. "We know who. Gloria Wilcox."

Amster looked surprised. "Yes, Ms. Wilcox. I have sold a number of her silk screens to a gentleman—fifteen of them, I believe. He's asked for confidentiality, and, of course, I must respect that. Perhaps he's had some luck with them in Europe. He doesn't report to me, you know."

Henny went on. "We have reports of resales of her work going for as high as fifteen thousand bucks."

Amster's eyes popped.

"I had no idea! I'm certainly not selling them for that much—a tenth of that. We still have two of her works on display."

"We checked them out," Henny said.

Amster continued to share his astonishment as the door of the rear office opened and produced Mildred again.

"Darling, the gentleman who bought the fifteen silk screens seems to be reselling them for fifteen thousand dollars each overseas. What do you think?"

Then, in a shocking development, Mildred spoke.

"How nice for him." She sashayed past us out into the gallery.

"Nothing upsets, Mildred," Amster explained, smiling. "Wonderful girl. Keeps me grounded."

And irons his kilts, I thought. I had a question. "Did you tell the fellow who bought the silk screens there had been complaints about poor dealing?"

"No. Never actually met the man. He may have been in the gallery to look them over, but if he was, he never made himself known to me. He bought over the internet. Paid for shipping. Ms. Wilcox made a tidy sum."

Susan looked from Henny to me.

"Anything else?" she asked.

Henny and I asked all we needed to. Everyone rose, shook hands, and thanked one another. Amster bustled to the door, his kilt whirling in his gracious haste, and showed us through the gallery, giving a shout to his darling Mildred, who waved good-bye and threw kisses from a far corner. He showed us the stairway down, and off we three went into the evening.

Seventeen

The new day did not change the opinion Henny, Susan, and I had formed the night before. Whitney Amster struck us as an honest man—within reasonable parameters. The business he ran may have been a tad predatory, feeding on the airy dreams of hopeful artists, but, strictly speaking, not dishonest. His explanation of the European price mark-up, as well as his apparent distance from it… the way he offered up information without our having to gouge it out of him… his lack of guilty tics and tells… even his insouciant relationship with Mildred all added up, in our six eyes, to no involvement in whatever was happening with Gloria Wilcox's art work. That being true, it meant no one in the art world had any motive for knocking off Alania Simpson. So, why the hell did someone knock her off? We'd come to these conclusions over drinks the night before after leaving Amster's gallery. With the three of us concurring, we had to be right.

Henny had given Gloria a late call after we'd reached our conclusions and set up an appointment with her in our office after school the next day—today. Henny and I sat all day long sporadically discussing what we needed to talk to Gloria about. Henny took one more crack in front of the mirror at making sense of Sam Spade's wriggling attempts to display anger. I convinced him to cut it out. Someone might walk in on us at any time, and if he were contorting and shimmying in front of a mirror, they'd walk right out again. At three twenty-five we heard the clanking of our elevator. I expected Gloria Wilcox to walk through our door, but Detective Thursday did instead, and he didn't look happy. He flopped into our client chair, uninvited.

"How'd you guys entertain yourselves last evening?" A smug smile sat on his face.

Henny opened his desk drawer slowly. Thursday's brow furrowed then relaxed when Henny extracted a toothpick.

"We took in the world of art. But you know that," Henny replied, casually unbuttoning his gray, double-breasted jacket as if he didn't have a care in the world.

"I asked you mugs to leave police work to the police."

Henny removed his toothpick and pointed it at the detective. "We don't think the sale of art work had anything to do with the lady getting bumped off."

A look of comical disgust replaced the smug smile on Thursday's face.

"Is that right? Heh! So you know, we've got Interpol working on the case as well as the New York City police department. Glad to hear you're butting out, though."

"You misheard. I didn't say we were butting out," Henny replied.

I swear I could hear the word flatfoot coming at me telepathically after every comment Henny made to Thursday. The phone rang.

"Gotta get this," Henny said. Thursday and I waited. "Yeah, no problem. Our calendar's clear for the rest of the day. Take your time. We'll wait." He hung up.

It sounded like Gloria Wilcox was running late. I was glad Gloria Wilcox was running late. I'd been afraid she'd walk in right in the middle of our discussion with Thursday, and the situation would increase in its stickiness.

Thursday took up the thread. "There ain't nothing to investigate if you ain't investigating the art angle."

Henny shrugged. I felt useless, spectating, so I jumped in.

"We have another angle we're looking into, Detective."

Thursday rose. "Good, you do that. Looks like I made this trip for nothing. You two aren't going to be any problem." He left the office without a backward glance. This time he closed the door.

"I'm gonna solve this case or die," Henny muttered.

"Gloria Wilcox before?"

"Yeah. She'll be here four thirty or so."

"Good thing our calendar's clear, eh?"

Henny grunted, and we went back to waiting.

Not until four forty-five did I hear the elevator clank its way to the third floor. A moment later, a tearful Gloria Wilcox joined us. I rose and helped her into our client chair, presuming the visit to our office had rekindled the heartbreak of her friend's death.

I took my seat and waited for Gloria to compose herself. When she did, she didn't say anything near what I expected.

"He's a monster, a little monster. Oh, if you only knew how much of a monster he is."

Henny and I glanced at one another.

"Who is?" I asked.

"Victor Figueroa."

Henny and I glanced at one another again.

"Who is Victor Figueroa?"

"He's a little monster."

We were getting nowhere. "Does this have anything to do with your friend's death?"

"Another day like today, he'll have something to do with my death. Ha! Alania's probably happy where she is; happy she no longer has to deal with the little monstrosity."

Henny piped in. "Ms. Wilcox, would you like a little drink to settle your nerves?"

"Drink? You have drinks here? Where?"

Henny produce the Boone's That's All and a paper cup. Gloria threw it back like a longshoreman. Her rueful glance into the empty cup induced Henny to pour her another. This, she sipped.

"Oh," Gloria sighed heavily. "I'm sorry to be late, but Victor Figueroa…"

Henny couldn't resist the allure of Boone's That's All, so he poured himself a drink and another for me. He waggled the bottle toward Gloria, and she held out her half-filled cup. We were admirably set for the long haul.

"What did you want to see me about?" Gloria asked.

Henny gestured my way, the Boone's That's All now his priority.

"I think we have some good news for you," I said, "if you could call it that."

"Good, I need some."

"We do not believe your art work had anything to do with your friend's death. Her championing you was simply a coincidence."

"Well, why was she murdered then?"

"We haven't quite gotten that far yet. We wanted to ask whether you could give us any more information about Ms. Simpson. Something in her personal life, perhaps? A scorned lover? Money problems?"

"No, no money problems. She loaned me money, you recall, and made it back plus some. We never talked much about men. We are…were long past the age where men are constantly on our mind."

"Problems in school?" I suggested. I didn't see how a murder could spring from that, but I couldn't think of anything else.

"Only that little son-of-a-bitch Victor Figueroa."

"A supervisor?"

"Ha! Not even supervisors rival him. No, he's a sadistic little eight-year-old."

The description stopped me cold and got Henny's attention.

"Why's he such a horror? He can't be that bad," Henny asked.

"Ha! He runs around the room at will; he talks, yells out curses whenever he feels like it; he calls me Mrs. Suckcox; he hurts the other children… name it, he's guilty. Today, he comes to art with his class, grabs a bottle of yellow finger paint and starts smearing it on kids' desks. The kids go nuts and start laughing and screaming. Who gets in trouble? Victor Figueroa, public enemy number one? No, of course not. I do—for not being able to control the class. Who can control a monster like him? I only have him one period a week. Poor Alania. She had him all day, every day. I don't know how she stood it. I could give you a list a yard long of the mayhem he's caused."

"Doesn't the school contact his parents?" I asked.

"Ha! Like the parents care. They've given up. They can't do anything with him. They've beaten him—he's come to school with bruises, but does it help? No! It only makes him worse. Alania reported the family to Children's Services for child abuse. She joked she'd call it pest control, not child abuse. But she reported it. And more than once. She called them; she wrote them."

"What came of it?" I asked.

"I don't know. She reported him in early October. It's been, what, two months? I was late getting here because the school called the father about today's eruption, and I had to be there. The father's as big a nut as the kid."

"Why so?" Henny asked.

"I think he arrived drunk. He smelled drunk. He acted drunk. And does he talk to the kid? No, just rants and raves about the school not taking away his son from him. He'll never permit it, and they'd better not try it. Blah blah blah."

"The school can do that?" Henny asked.

"No. I told you. Alania reported the family to Children's Services. The school can give evidence. I mean school's where the kid spends his day, interacts with human beings who aren't members of his nut case family. It's where he acts out the most. The little creep is uncontrollable."

"And he's only eight years old?" Henny asked.

"Ha!" Gloria ha!-ed again. "If you knew the amount of evil that could fit into one eight year old, you'd have your tubes tied."

I didn't bother to point out the biological impossibility involved. "And you say Alania started this procedure?"

"When she found out last June the kid was going to be in her class, she looked into the procedure for reporting. She expected things to go haywire. The kid is a two-legged machine for aging and destroying teachers, and she wanted to be ready."

"I wonder how far the procedure had moved along," Henny said.

Gloria tossed back her Boone's That's All.

"I don't know," she said. "All that stuff is hush hush confidential." She put her empty cup on Henny's desk. "I feel much better now. Thank you."

I didn't wonder after two and half shots of Boone's.

Gloria rose and Henny offered to walk her to the elevator. When he returned, he said, "I'm meeting Gloria later."

"What does that mean?"

"She lives on Sixth Street North in Greenpoint. I can walk it in half an hour from our building."

I was perplexed. "Shouldn't you keep the affairs of the heart separate from your professional duties?"

Henny frowned. "Your anatomy may be geographically faulty, but she kind of gets to me."

"She's gotta be ten years older than you. At least."

"The heart has no eyes," he said, offering me a cavalier wave of the hand.

"Yeah, but the head has eyes. Never mind." Let Henny be Henny was my motto. He left shortly afterward. I had nowhere to go, so I sat in the office. Susan said she'd call after we interviewed Gloria, and at six o'clock, she did. I filled Susan in on Detective Thursday's visit and on how little help Gloria was in moving the motive for the murder away from the art world. I felt a tad jealous of Henny, out in the world with a woman, so I offered to buy Susan a Mexican dinner. She accepted, and we agreed to meet on the street in front of my office building in half an hour.

I straightened up the office. The bottle of Boone's That's All still sat on Henny's desk, but I exercised considerable self-control and put it back into his drawer, although only a drink or two remained in it. My mood was good, thanks to the earlier encounter with the Boone's, and I looked forward to mixing some tequila with it, hoping the combination wouldn't be overly combustible.

The chill air felt good when I left the building. I had a few minutes, so I walked to the end of the block, crossed over, and walked back up the block. I always got a charge out of seeing our sign in the third-floor window, still visible in the light of the street lamp. There was Mayor de Blasio smiling down on me from above, and I gave him a nod. I crossed back to my side of the street and had a thought. I re-entered our building's lobby and looked over the glass-enclosed directory hanging on the wall. From the fourth floor to the tenth, all city agencies. Room 714—Children's Services. I wondered whether they'd be able to tell me anything about Victor Figueroa's case. I figured since it was only a clanking ride on our elevator, I'd make a visit next day.

Susan saw me in the lobby gazing at the directory and knocked on the door. We greeted one another fondly and headed off to Casa de Grande for dinner.

Next morning, I went to Children's Services first thing, but got nowhere. Gloria was right. Hush hush confidential ruled the day—even after I flashed my PI license.

Henny got in late, something unusual for him. He looked frazzled.

"How was your evening?" I asked. "Susan and I went for Mexican."

Henny fell into his chair.

"That poor woman has to do what she does for about thirty more years until she can retire. Fifty-four hundred more workdays, she told me."

"She counted them?"

"Not counting sick days or snow days. After last night, I know Victor Figueroa better than I know you. The kid must be a real pip."

"She talked about him?"

"Endlessly. Until I got enough red wine into her to…uh…change the topic."

That moved us closer to a TMI moment, so I didn't pursue the conversation. Instead, I told Henny of my trip upstairs. He advised me to keep a safe distance from Victor F., but I'd grown curious. I called Gloria's school and managed to get an appointment with Mr. Miralax, the principal, for one o'clock.

A little before one, I sat in the school office waiting for permission to enter the principal's inner sanctum, when I heard screaming from outside in the hallway. A young boy ran into the office, scrambled up onto the counter dividing the workspace from the wait space. The boy took off one of his shoes and hurled it at the secretary, who sat at her desk thirty feet away watching the spectacle. She batted the shoe away, a weary look on her face. The boy on the countertop screeched in a manner Tarzan would have envied from his hut on the escarpment. The principal's door snapped open and a short, balding man, Mr. Miralax, I presumed, popped into view.

"Oh, Victor," he said. "Not you again." The man's shoulders slumped in defeat. "Down. Get down from there. Do you want me to call your father again?"

"He don't care." The boy took off his other shoe and sent in flying toward Mr. Miralax, who didn't even bother to move aside. The shoe hit him in the shoulder.

"Now, how are you going to go home with no shoes on?" Mr. Miralax asked. The boy unsnapped his pants and started to remove them, but this crossed a line for Mr. Miralax. He strode to the counter, grabbed Victor around the waist, and grounded him. The boy broke free and charged into Mr. Miralax's office.

"Oh, no you don't." Mr. Miralax sounded his battle cry. "Get me Dashawn," he cried over his shoulder to the secretary as he followed the boy into the office and closed the door behind him. Strange noises issued from the office. The secretary's eyes met mine.

"This happen often?" I asked.

"More than you'd think," she said, picking up the phone.

A few moments later the office door opened, and Mr. Miralax's voice shouted, "Shoe."

The secretary got up and walked to the door. She didn't enter, but simply tossed the shoe inside.

"It's safer out here," she said to me and returned to her desk and her reports.

Another spate of odd noises came from the office, and a security guard walked past me. The guard, tall, young, and uniformed, with the nametag D. Greene, went directly into the principal's office and a moment later came out, holding hands with a quiet Victor.

"Let's get ice cream today," Victor was saying.

I couldn't take my eyes off the boy.

"What are you looking at?" the youngster asked.

"Nothing. Sorry," I apologized. The kid scared me. I heard my name. Mr. Miralax beckoned. I entered the office and helped pick up two overturned chairs. I sat at the short side of a rectangular table, Miramax nearby at the long side. "Sorry about the commotion," he said.

"Uh, your tie," I pointed out. The man's tie lay off near his right shoulder. He felt for it and brought it back over his shirt buttons.

"What can I do for you?"

"I'm investigating the death of one of your teachers. Alania Simpson."

"Oh, yes. Terrible thing. I'll never recover from the news."

As Mr. Miralax mopped beads of sweat from his forehead, it struck me there were numerous things he might never recover from.

"Tell me," I said. "Was that the little boy from Ms. Simpson's class—Victor Figueroa?"

Miramax's shoulders slumped again. "That's him. That's him. Poor Ms. Simpson had to put up with him day after day. He was a handful last year but not like this. I can't even imagine next year."

Mr. Miralax seemed eager to talk about what I wanted to talk about, so I helped him along.

"I understand she referred him, the boy and his family, to Children's Services."

"Oh, lord. She was in my office almost every day asking what the delay was in doing something about him. We had the father in repeatedly. Asked for his help. Offered assistance. Even threatened him."

"Threatened him how?"

"We mentioned the bruises on the boy. He claimed he was trying to discipline Victor for our benefit."

"And the threat?"

"Mrs. Simpson pointed out to Mr. Figueroa more than once that Children's Services had the authority to remove the child from the home for the safety of the child—not to mention the safety of the children in his class and the school and everyone's sanity."

"Did Mr. Figueroa take the threat seriously?"

"Oh, did he! From that point on the only thing he wanted to talk about was my arrogance, Ms. Simpson's arrogance, in treating him that way. Victor was his son and would never be taken from him and on and on and on. Dashawn seems to be the only one the boy'll listen to."

"The security guard?"

"Yes."

"I presume Mr. Figueroa and Ms. Simpson did not get along."

"Shouting matches, the worst I've ever seen. He was very angry with her, especially when she threatened him, as I said. I had to get Dashawn in here to escort Mr. Figueroa out."

"Can you tell me how far the process of removing Victor had progressed? In general terms without breeching confidentiality." I strove to appear reasonable.

"They'd interviewed the father and me. I know that much."

"Did they interview Ms. Simpson?"

"I know she wrote them, but, no, I don't think they ever got to interview her. She would've had to take a day off from school. I did. The morning, at least. I'd have known about it if she did. After her death, Children's Services said we needed to place the child in another class with an established teacher to give the boy a fresh opportunity. You see the good it did. Everything's up in the air now."

I had pretty much all I thought I needed. I thanked Mr. Miralax and went back to the office. I explained everything I had in mind to Henny, and we talked it over and came to a unified conclusion. He petitioned me to allow him to make the call to Detective Thursday. I figured Henny needed a positive experience after his previous, trying evening with Gloria Wilcox, so I let him.

He lifted the phone, then put it down.

"Are you sure we got it right?" Henny asked me.

"I told you all I know. Speak now or forever hold your peace."

Henny nodded slowly. "We're smarter than any bone-weary numb-nuts police dick, right?"

It didn't seem to me we had been yet, but in for a penny….

"No doubt about it," I agreed.

He made the call, and Thursday promised to stop in between four and six.

Eighteen

Henny set up a code with me. If he put his toothpick into his mouth, I needed to take up the thread of the narrative. If the toothpick was out, he had the floor. At five-fifteen, Detective Thursday sashayed into the office, cutting a look of utter disdain in two and giving Henny and me each half.

"Don't ask me why, but my lieutenant told me to follow up with you two nimrods. What d'ya want?"

Henny took a toothpick from the drawer, clutched it between two fingers, and launched our rocket.

"You're all wrong…" I tensed as I sensed the word "flatfoot" in the ether. Thankfully, it remained there. "…pal, about having an art angle to your murder case. We told you that before."

"I walked over here for this again? You think you know more than us and Interpol combined, eh?"

"You get anything back from Interpol?"

Thursday's jaw jutted.

"Not yet."

Henny waved the back of his toothpick hand and offered an airy, "Pfft."

"Here's what went down," he said.

Henny didn't need me at all. He carefully spun the tale as I'd explained it to him. I listened, on the edge of spellbound, even though I knew the plot. Henny was good. I'd hoped to invite Susan to the unveiling, as it were, but she'd been sent up to Albany for the weekend to interview some people about a municipal corruption scandal and left a couple hours earlier. As Henny narrated, Thursday's brow creased into thoughtful lines. He didn't interrupt. He hurled no snide asides into Henny's airspace. Not a peep came out of him.

"You know what to do now? Where to look? Who to collar?" Henny concluded.

I studied Thursday. He seemed uncomfortable but…'enriched' would, I think, be the proper word. He would be leaving with much more than he brought.

Henny lowered his voice. "As a gesture of good will, though I don't know you deserve it…"

A flash of cold crossed Thursday's face. "…the credit for the case is all yours. Leave us out. We might need one another's help someday down the road. What do you say?"

Thursday rose. "I say I'll look into it, and that's all I'll say." Thursday clearly, to my eye, pondered whether to break his word immediately and say something more. He paused at the office door.

"I will let you know what comes of it. One way or the other."

I figured Thursday would prefer the "other," just to have another chance to lambast us about keeping our noses out of police business.

An anxious weekend passed, and we heard nothing from him. Early Monday morning our phone rang, and Henny picked up.

"Yeah. Yeah. We'll be here. You a drinking man?" Henny looked my way. "He hung up."

"Who?"

"Who do you think? Thursday. He's coming right over."

"What'd he say?"

"He said he's coming right over."

"How'd he sound?"

"Gruff."

"Gruff?"

"Gruff."

"He always sounds gruff."

"Then he sounded like he always sounds."

"You weren't thinking of offering him some Boone's, were you?"

Henny shrugged. "Why not? Seal the bond."

I doubted we'd be sealing anything today except our own dismal fate if I'd gotten things wrong.

Twenty minutes later, Thursday arrived. I thought I detected a smidge of humility in both his walk and the gentle way in which he lowered himself into our client chair.

"It kills me to say this," he began. "But I gotta hand it to you. You nailed it. Murder solved; case closed."

Thursday's deflated, yet prideful, recounting of what happened after he left our office on Friday filled my heart with glee. I'd never seen Henny arch an individual eyebrow before and didn't even know he could, but he did it multiple times as he munched on a toothpick.

"Glad to help," Henny said nonchalantly as Thursday concluded his tale. "And I hope you left us out of it?"

"I did. But I'll remember."

"That's all I want. Too early for a drink?"

Thursday frowned. "Yeah, way too early. I gotta get back to the precinct." He rose. "Have a good week. You got my card, right?"

"Got it," Henny said, patting the top desk drawer. "And you got our number, right?"

Thursday slapped his left buttock, a gesture which had no other meaning, I hoped, than that's where he kept his wallet and our card.

Henny spun his chair in my direction.

"Nice work, pardner."

"Can't wait to give the story to Susan." She was due back in town that afternoon. "I'm gonna text her to come here right from the train station."

When, at four o'clock, I heard the elevator and caught a silhouette at our door, I expected Susan to walk in, but it was Gloria Wilcox who graced our office with an appearance. I threw Henny a look.

"I invited Gloria," he explained. "She deserves to know what happened, too. I told her a little over the phone."

Gloria entered, toting things. In one hand she held a large rectangle wrapped in what looked like butcher paper. In the other, clearly a bottle of something. She handed the bottle to Henny who lifted out a sparkling new supply of Boone's That's All. She handed me the wrapped rectangle. I removed the paper and unveiled a silk screen of the Twin Towers. "This, too," Gloria added. She handed me a check for a thousand dollars. "I want you both to have these. One permanent—for your office; the other two for as long as they last. I hope the check is big enough."

"Don't worry about the check," Henny said. "I'm sure it's fine."

I folded the check quickly and pocketed it.

"Henny told me you'd solved the case, and I had nothing to do with it. I'm so grateful. And relieved."

The elevator clanked again, and a moment later, Susan entered, rolling a suitcase behind her. I grabbed a folding wooden chair from the closet, and we mixed and mingled for a moment. Henny extracted the paper cups from hiding, emptied our old bottle of Boone's and cracked open the new one.

Susan graciously offered the more comfortable client chair to Gloria and said, "So, give me the scoop. If I can deliver my story by eight, you're in the paper tomorrow."

Henny'd insisted, with fairness on his side and justice on mine, that since he had center stage with Detective Thursday, I could have the spotlight for the two ladies.

"The story's not long, nor is it complicated. Alania Simpson had been having a ton of trouble with the kid I told you about, this Victor Figueroa." I addressed this to Susan. "The school principal, a Mr. Miralax, told me she and the boy's father engaged in screaming matches. The father was afraid the city would take the kid away from him, and he blamed Alania."

"Why he would want him at all, I'll never know," Gloria interrupted.

"At any rate, according to Detective Thursday, Mr. Figueroa spent the early part of the day in question at a bar on Madison Street. The bartender said his rage over the whole situation ratcheted up as he downed the alcohol. He left the bar promising to give Alania Simpson a piece of his mind. He went to the school and saw Alania walking down the street on her way here to tell Henny and me about your art problem. Figueroa followed her. He'd already been called to Children's Service for an interview. Unfortunately, the office that summoned him is four floors over our heads. When he saw Alania closing in on this building, maybe even pausing in the lobby to check the directory for the number of our office, Figueroa presumed she was going to Children's Services in person to report on him again. He had a gun, a twenty-two; he used it. Alania managed to make it to our front door but no farther. Thursday tracked down Figueroa's movements that day; found the gun in his apartment; matched ballistics; even got a tearful confession from Figueroa about protecting the rights of his son. There you have it. I'd interview Thursday if you want to flesh it out, Susan."

"My art did have something to do with it. If…"

"Only on the far periphery," I said in what I hoped was a soothing manner. "Figueroa was coming after Alania, no matter. He was drunk. If he'd gone into the school in his inebriated rage and with a gun, who knows what might have happened, and who might have gotten hurt."

Neither the ladies nor I had sipped from our paper cups while I spoke, but now we did.

"And you got on to Mr. Figueroa how?" Susan asked.

"Talking to the principal. Plus, with Mayor de Blasio's face smiling down from above, I already knew this building was full of city offices. I wanted to check with Children's Service about the boy, and there was Children's Services right in our building. They wouldn't tell me anything, and that sent me to the school principal. On that day, at that moment, Figueroa just happened to be drunk; just happened to follow Alania; she just happened to be coming to the same building where he'd been interviewed about his kid; he just happened to be carrying his little gun. A perfect storm of mortal misfortune."

"Can I use that?" Susan asked.

"Use what?"

"Your 'perfect storm of mortal misfortune'?"

"Be my guest."

Henny interjected.

"We gave the glory of the solve to Detective Thursday. You do that, too. Don't mention anything about us."

"Really?" Susan asked, skeptically.

"Henny's way of ingratiating ourselves with the police," I explained. "Mutual benefit and aid society. And, no, you can't use 'mutual benefit and aid society.'"

Susan smiled and said, "A celebration is in order, don't you think? Giando on the Water? Gloria, do you think we might treat the boys for giving me a good story and for clearing your conscience?"

"Absolutely. I've been to Giando's. The chicken rollatini is to die for."

"Let's all meet there at eight," Susan suggested. "And wear your tuxedos. Have you seen them?" she asked Gloria. "Very dashing. Is eight too late?"

"I'll go home, pretty up, and take an Uber," Gloria said, rising.

Susan rose with her. "And I have to get to Detective Thursday and write up my story. Not too much…" She waggled her finger at the nearly full bottle of Boone's.

The ladies left, and Henny and I settled back.

"What do you think?" Henny asked, tapping the Boone's bottle. "We got a little time."

"So we do. Why not?"

So we drank, but only once, and that, a short one.

187

Nineteen

The Missing Black Bird

A quiet week preceded a quiet weekend. We'd gotten two phone calls and three internet nibbles, but nothing came of them. As the next Monday unfolded with nothing to do, Henny commented on our successes of the three months we'd been detecting. We each had our own apartment, even though if apartments had an evolutionary ladder, we'd be ranked at the unicellular stage. We each had a low, four-digit bank account, (six if you count the two digits after the decimal point) and the office had a low, four-digit bank account. Another case or two to end the current year, and we'd sail into the new year in fine shape. Shortly after three o'clock, we heard our elevator.

Henny held up his right hand, fingers crossed. Two silhouettes appeared behind our frosted glass door window. Then a knock. I got up and let in two people, one an older woman, finely dressed and holding a handbag that appeared to be expensive since it had someone's initials embroidered or tattooed into it in gold letters. Accompanying her was a young girl, dressed primly. Instead of an expensive handbag, she carried a small stuffed bear, blue in color.

"Henny and Lloyd's establishment, I believe?" the woman said. "I've been referred by Mrs. von Schneiderhoven, whom I believe you know."

"Yes, of course we do," Henny said, rising and gesturing in the direction of our client chair.

"Where am I supposed to sit?" the girl asked.

"Lloyd," Henny said.

I got a folding chair out of the closet and set it up.

"On that?" the girl asked. "It's not very fancy. Bippy likes fancy stuff." Bippy was the blue bear. "This whole place isn't very fancy."

"Ashley Mae," the woman chastised. "My granddaughter. She never knew her mother. Very sad story. I've spoiled her, I'm afraid."

"Not enough," the girl muttered. She stared at Henny. "Why are you dressed like that?" She looked my way. "Why's he dressed like that?"

"Like what?" I asked. The woman took a seat.

"He looks like the fancy, dressed up wolf in cartoons I watch. Is that a shoot suit?" The girl threw back her head and laughed.

"A shoot suit?" Henny asked.

The girl explained. "Yeah, you know. The big hat and twirling your watch around, making eyes at girls." She made a face, thrust out her hip, made believe she twirled a watch and chain, and leered at Henny and me. "Hubba hubba," she finished.

"Shoot suit. Oh!" I exclaimed. "A zoot suit." I smiled at the girl. "I've seen those cartoons. They don't make them like that anymore."

"Why should they?" Ashley Mae asked. "They already made them?"

"Uh, well." She stumped me. "You make a good point."

"So? Why's he dressed like a cartoon?"

Henny defended himself. "I'm not dressed like a cartoon. Notice the lapels? Not nearly as wide as a zoot suit. Do you see me swinging a watch around?" He pulled up his sleeve to show his wristwatch.

"Do you look at girls? I'll bet you do."

"I don't say hubba hubba."

"Ashley Mae, please. Hush," her grandmother ordered.

"Why don't you take a seat, Ashley, you and Boopy?" Henny said.

"Bippy, not Boopy," Ashley corrected, giving Henny a look of profound sympathy. "And my name is Ashley Mae." She walked off to inspect the office.

Henny's glare followed her.

"Henny," I said softly, recalling him. I addressed the woman. "May we know your name?"

"Yes. I am Deidre Delangersfeld."

The woman did not pause, but I do for a moment to give you an appreciation of the effect her next words had on Henny. His bucket list decreased by one, you'll recall, when he got to work on a murder case. A second item, perhaps the only other thing on his list, would now be satisfied, at least partially, when the woman said:

"My black bird has been stolen."

I heard Henny's sharp intake of breath.

"Say it again," he ordered Mrs. Delangersfeld, who from here on will be called Deirdre. Where do these women get these names?

"I say my black bird has been stolen. I want you to find it."

Henny, a beatific look on his face, slid open his top desk drawer and pulled out his copy of *The Maltese Falcon*. The cover showed a statuette of a black falcon.

"Does it look like this?" Henny asked, the excitement in his voice palpable.

"Certainly not," Deidre huffed. Ashley Mae hustled over to take a peek at the book cover.

"That's not a real bird," Ashley Mae pointed out with some disdain. "Twinky's a real bird, a meat bird, not a make-believe statue. He flies and everything." Ashley Mae moved her hand through the air, to explain flying to Henny.

Deirdre continued. "He was stolen, cage and all, and I want you to do something about it."

"It's hot in here," Ashley Mae interrupted.

"Take your coat off," Henny snapped.

"There's no place to put it," Ashley Mae complained.

Henny pointed to our coat tree, where his fedora and our two coats hung.

"I can't reach. Is that your shoot suit hat? It's awful little. The wolf had a bigger one."

Henny stood and moved Ashley Mae's chair over to the windows.

"Put your coat on the back of the chair. Sit here and watch the cars go by," he advised. "It's great fun. Boopy'll love it."

"Bippy, not Boopy! Is that what you do for fun?" Ashley Mae asked. "It's dumb."

"Ashley Mae, please," Deirdre commanded. "We have business to conduct here. How can I get Twinky back if you keep interrupting?"

"I don't know," Ashley Mae said, pouting. She took the chair and held Bippy up to the window. "He doesn't like it. He thinks it's stupid."

Henny ignored the girl and returned to his seat.

"Now," he said, "details. You said the bird is black. A real bird?"

"A crow. A trained crow."

"She talks to Twinky all night long," Ashley Mae interjected from her window seat.

"He's very bright," Deirdre explained.

"Smarter than me, probably," Ashley Mae said.

"I wouldn't say that, darling," Deirdre contended.

"Close," Ashley Mae argued.

"Mrs. Delangersfeld, we'll never get anywhere with these interruptions," Henny said curtly.

"Yes, Ashley Mae. Now stop interrupting."

"Sure, who cares what I think?"

"Shhh!" Deirdre shushed. "Twinky had a lovely cage to rest in. I left his cage door open until bedtime. He often came to sit on my shoulder. He knew enough to return to his cage to eat and to…uh…"

"Poop," Ashley Mae added. "The word is poop."

"Ashley Mae! Stop. At any rate, Mr. Henny, Mr. Lloyd, that gives you an idea of the bird's intelligence. He never made any trouble, never…embarrassed himself, if you will."

"Never pooped on the floor, she means."

"Ashley Mae! Please! Saturday afternoon, I picked Ashley Mae up from dance class after I finished my shopping, came home, and he was gone. The cage was gone. Simply gone. Someone got into the townhouse and out again with the bird. Oh, I miss him dreadfully."

I'd stayed quiet long enough.

"This past Saturday?" I asked.

"Yes, two days ago. In the afternoon."

"Did you call the police?" I asked.

"Big help they were. They came because I said I'd been robbed. They couldn't wait to leave after I told them the nature of the robbery. They promised to keep an eye out. I poured my heart out over my loss to my good friend Mrs. von Schneiderhoven, and she suggested I contact the two of you. Well?"

I knew perfectly well that chasing down this sort of black bird was not the dream-come-true case Henny longed for, but from his answer, I guess he realized it might be the only black bird he'd ever have a chance to recover.

"We'll take the case," Henny said.

"Oh, thank you. I'm so relieved."

"We'll need to inspect the scene of the crime," Henny pointed out.

"By all means. Would you like to come home with us now?"

Ashley Mae sauntered over.

"Yeah," she said. "Come home with us. I'll show you what you look like as a cartoon."

Henny made eye contact with the girl and in return received a phony smile and a sarcastic waggle of her head.

"How old are you, little girl?" Henny asked.

"Eight. And my name is Ashley Mae."

"Eight," Henny muttered. He turned to me. "Another eight-year-old," and faintly added, "I think I would have my tubes tied."

We left the office and crowded into Deirdre's car, which had been waiting downstairs, and off we went to the Upper East Side.

The townhouse sat a block off the river on a tree-lined street which had two speed bumps, each a third of the way from the end of the block. I didn't see a school anywhere nearby, so I figured somebody had to know somebody to get their street so especially protected. Deirdre led us inside, pulling Ashley Mae along by the hand. A woman, apparently alerted to our arrival, opened the door for us. We handed her our coats, and she took them and Ashley Mae off to some other part of the house. Henny and I followed Deirdre into a very spiffy living room. It wasn't as large as Arabella von Schneiderhoven's living room, but Henny's and my apartments could have been cozily been tucked into opposite corners of the room with plenty of space left over for a cotillion or two.

"Right there," Deirdre said, pointing.

Henny and I walked over to the window, where a bird cage stand stood bare and useless. Henny and I peeked at one another, and we made a show of inspecting the stand.

"Do you see anything?" Deirdre asked.

We didn't. What could we possibly see?

Henny ran his hand up and down the pole of the stand. Why, I had no idea.

"So," he said, "the bird was in the cage, and all the thief had to do was lift the cage off and go out the door?"

"Presumably. Twinky is allowed free access to the house. I believe I mentioned that as well as the reasons for it."

The no-poop situation, as I recalled.

"He must have flown back into the cage for food or, ahem, something else, of course."

"I see," Henny said, looking past Deirdre and scowling. Ashley Mae had entered the room.

"You find him yet?" she asked, meeting Henny's leery gaze with one of her own.

Henny played the grown-up, though, and ignored the challenge. I felt proud of him.

"So, you were shopping and the kid was at dance class?" Henny asked.

"My name is Ashley Mae," the kid said.

"Quiet, Ashley Mae," Deirdre ordered. "Yes."

"Are you sure you locked the front door? Where was the woman who took our coats? Who else had keys to the house?"

"I'm certain I locked the door. Doris does not work on weekends, and nobody has keys to the house but me and her, but she's been with me for fifteen years."

"Longer than me even," Ashley Mae pointed out.

"Ashley Mae, will you hush?" her grandmother scolded.

"What does Doris do around here?" Henny asked.

"She takes Ashley Mae to school and other places she needs to go during the week. Picks her up after school; helps her with her homework."

"I don't need help. I'm smartest in the class," Ashley Mae corrected.

"Doris does some cleaning, cooking, runs errands on occasion. She a wonderful woman."

"Did the kid go to school today?" Henny asked, giving Ashley Mae a sideways glance.

"Ashley Mae," the girl said, her inflection rising.

"Of course. I picked her up after school today, and we came right to your office. I wanted Doris here to guard the scene of the crime for you. Besides, I was worried Ashley Mae might be too distressed by this tragedy. She would need her grandmother with her if she were."

Ashley Mae mumbled the word "tragedy" and gave a quick roll of her eyes.

"Did you receive a ransom note or a ransom phone call?" I asked.

"Ransom! My word. No, of course not. You think Twinky might be kidnapped for ransom?"

"No, not if no one has contacted you," I pointed out. I beckoned Henny, and we stepped aside. "What do you think?"

"The old lady's told us what she knows. We'll have to talk to Doris and the dance school the kid goes to."

"Why the dance school?"

"The kid may have mentioned the house being empty. Someone may have heard and slipped in to take the bird."

"Why the hell would anyone want to take a pet bird? And how would they get in?"

"We're detectives, Lloyd. We'll find out."

Henny's confidence was inspiring, but the likelihood of things panning out our way seemed extremely dubious to me. A house full of fancy stuff and somebody takes a bird? If true, then a lunatic prowled the neighborhood.

I realized we'd failed to ask an obvious question.

"Mrs. Delangersfeld, was anything else stolen?"

"Nothing that I can tell."

I leaned into Henny. "We should try pet stores; see if anyone's tried to sell a caged crow."

"Good idea," Henny agreed. "Ma'am, since we're here, may we take the opportunity to talk to Doris?"

"Of course. I'll send her to you. Ashley Mae, come with me. Go play with Bippy."

"Do you want to see my shoot suit cartoon and see what you look like?" Ashley Mae asked Henny.

"No."

Ashley Mae glared at Henny and stuck out her tongue. Henny curled his upper lip at the girl but refrained from sticking out his tongue. I felt proud of his restraint again. Deirdre marched her out, and a minute later, Doris bustled into the room.

Twenty

"You or me?" I whispered to Henny.

"You do it. The little kid annoys me."

I didn't entirely see what one had to do with the other, but I led the questioning.

"Doris…may I call you Doris? I'm afraid I don't know your la.st name."

00

Doris looked about fifty with streaks of gray in her short hair. I felt a motherly aura emanating from her.

"Doris is fine."

"You know Mrs. Delangersfeld's hired us to find the bird, if we can."

Doris nodded.

"You didn't work this past Saturday, right?"

"No, I have weekends off. I was home."

"Do you live alone?"

"No, with my husband."

"You have keys to the house, right?"

"I do. I keep them in my work purse."

"Your work purse?"

"Yes, if I had to switch them from purse to purse, I know I'd be forgetting them or leaving them in the wrong purse, so I use the same purse for work each day. Take the keys out to use them; put them back in when I'm done. Makes life easier."

"Your keys are never out of your purse?"

"Only when I lock or unlock the front door."

"Can you make any guess how someone might have gotten in to steal the bird?"

"No, not unless the door was left unlocked."

"Mrs. Delangersfeld says no."

Doris gave a perplexed shrug.

"Are you certain your keys were in your purse from Friday to Monday?"

"They were there on Friday. I didn't check on the keys over the weekend. I had no reason to. They were there today when I got here."

"Did you unlock the door this morning?"

"I usually unlock the door every morning. Mrs. Delangersfeld is bustling around with Ashley Mae, trying to get her ready for the day, so I let myself in."

"Only the two of them live here, correct?"

"Yes."

"And you take Ashley Mae to school."

"Yes. And pick her up."

"You said you usually unlock the door. Did you unlock it today?"

Doris took a moment.

"No," she answered. "Ashley Mae did. She greeted me with news of the theft."

"Was she upset?"

"It's difficult to tell with her. She threw herself into my arms. I held her and a short time afterward, I took her to school. She seemed fine."

"Henny?"

"I can't think of anything," Henny said. "Doris, would you ask Mrs. Delangersfeld to come back in here?"

"Happily." Doris left the room.

I faced Henny. "What'd'ya think?"

"Nothing strange in what she said. Ah, Mrs. Delangersfeld," Henny said. "Just a question or two. Did Doris unlock the front door today when she arrived?"

"Why, no. She usually does. I'm too busy fussing with Ashley Mae. She's a handful to get ready for school. I sometimes think she does it to annoy me."

"Who opened the door today?"

"Ashley Mae did. She looked for Doris from the window."

"And…"

"She told Doris about Twinky being stolen and hugged Doris, who comforted her."

"Then they went off to school?"

"Yes."

Henny looked thoughtful, and I wondered what he had in mind.

"We have some ideas," Henny said. "We'll be off now."

"Please, do everything you can. I beg you. Twinky means the world to me, the absolute world."

"We'll do our best," Henny promised, and we bade the woman farewell.

"Their two stories match. Looks like Doris told the truth."

"Why wouldn't she? Now what?" I asked, when we reached the sidewalk.

"Try to get a list of pet stores in the area. We're here; might as well check them out."

I googled pet stores along with the zip code and ended up with two choices. We could either look into the "Ten Best Pet Stores on the Upper East Side" according to Yelp or the four hundred seventy-three pet stores on the Upper East Side listed in the Yellow Pages site.

"Let's do the ten," Henny said. "You take five; I'll take five."

We found a bench, sat, and made the calls. Dogs, yes; cats, yes; parakeets, yes; snakes, ferrets, hamsters, gerbils, fish, yes. Twinky the black crow, no.

"I'm not sure I want to make another four hundred fifty phone calls," I said.

"Let's go back to the office and talk this over."

"No, wait. You got the address of the dance school Ashley Mae went to?" I asked.

Henny pulled out his pad.

"Yeah. Ninetieth Street."

"Only a couple blocks. Let's check on whether little Ashley spilled the beans about an empty house to anyone."

"You think they'll talk to us."

"Good point. Wait." I got Mrs. Delangersfeld on my cell and asked her to call ahead to the dance studio and request them to give us every cooperation. She agreed.

"You're a genius, Lloyd."

"Yeah, right. So are you."

We set out.

The dance studio, "Little Angels A-Twirl," was on the second floor above a karate school. Henny and I took the stairs. The studio door opened onto a large, square room with horizontal bars at stomach height attached to the walls. The bars probably have a name in the ballet world, but I'm not in the ballet world. They were simply horizontal bars to me. The walls were mirrored all around. Two classes full of little girls, each with one leg or the other up in the air, were going on at opposite ends of the large room. A not unattractive teacher in leotards walked over to us.

"Hi," I said. "I'd like to speak to Ms. Danielle. She's expecting us."

The young woman pointed to a corner office.

"Ms. Danielle?" Henny asked me.

"Delangersfeld mentioned her when I called."

We knocked and entered. Ms. Danielle appeared to have been a dancer some time ago. Still dancer-thin, I was certain she'd been cashing Social Security checks for at least a decade. She had long, silver hair.

"Ah yes," Ms. Danielle said. "You must be the bird men. Please, sit."

Henny and I took two plastic-covered, cushioned chairs in front of her desk.

"Now, what would you like to know?"

Henny gestured my way.

"You seem to know about the stolen bird."

"Yes. Oh, yes. I just hung up from Mrs. Delangersfeld. Quite attached to the bird, she tells me. Odd, don't you think?"

"Life's funny," I replied. "The little girl was here dancing when the theft occurred, and her grandmother was shopping. Do you know whether the girl might have mentioned the empty townhouse to anyone during her time here?"

"Even if she did, I don't see how it would matter. We had four classes going on then. An hour per class. We have no room for parents to hang around during the lessons. That's why we give recitals in the local school three times a year. The parents need to see what their little darlings have accomplished. And they'll pay to see it, too. Mrs. Delangersfeld dropped her granddaughter here. Ashley Mae spent the hour being grumpy, as usual, with her dance teacher. She saw no other adults and, naturally, the teachers were here the whole time."

"Grumpy?"

"Ashley Mae does not like dancing class, but her grandmother insists."

Ms. Danielle's explanation of the afternoon obliterated any other questions I might have conjured up.

"Henny?"

"Not much wiggle room there for any mischief to occur," he said.

Henny and I rose.

"Thank you, Ms. Danielle, for your help," I said.

"I fear my help was no help at all," she said, laughing lightly.

"The theft didn't come from here. That's pretty clear," Henny said when we reached the sidewalk. "Elimination of possibilities is an important step toward the truth."

I wondered what 1940's movie Henny'd stolen that line from, but I let it stand unquestioned as we took the subway back to the office. As we rode the train, we decided nothing could be gained from sitting in the office, so we continued to Williamsburg, promising one another we'd give the case considerable thought that evening.

I woke up next morning depressed. I arrived at the office depressed. Henny, already at his desk, of course, said things which depressed me further. He skipped a "good morning," as always.

"I talked to Gloria last night," he reported. "She liked the idea of checking pet shops. Whoever took the bird didn't take it because they loved crows. They think they can make money selling it."

"Unless they do love crows," I grunted.

"No way. I already made fifteen calls from that long list we found yesterday. No crows yet. You get a chance to talk to Susan?"

Talking to Susan is what had originally depressed me.

"Yes, I did."

"And?"

"She said we're looking for the bird backwards."

"What does that mean?"

I took very little pride in telling Henny what it meant, but I had to.

"She hung up on me last night and called back ten minutes later. Ten minutes! It took her ten minutes."

"Called back. Go on. What took her ten minutes?"

"Instead of looking for the crow, we needed to let the crow find us, she said. And it found her in ten minutes."

"Could you speed things up a little?"

"She went on Craig's List and found one pet crow for sale—cage included—in all of New York City. I have the number."

Henny had no response.

"Why didn't we think of doing that?" I asked.

Henny continued unresponsive.

"Can you call Deirdre? I don't think I have the strength," I said.

"Call her why?"

"Ask her to describe the cage in detail. A crow is a crow, I presume, but the cage may have distinguishing characteristics."

Henny made the call and listened to a description of the cage, which he passed on to me. Only two details stood out. The cage was extra large, and it had Twinky's name posted under the cage door on a metal strip. I had Henny make another call, and he left a message. Mildred Almadovar called back while we ate lunch. We made an appointment for three o'clock to see the bird.

Mildred lived in a low-rise apartment complex on Avenue H, near Brooklyn College. On the train ride to Brooklyn, Henny and I discussed in great detail how to handle this. Mildred buzzed us into the building, and we found the first floor apartment easily. Mildred welcomed us at her door, and Henny took the lead.

"May we see the bird?" he asked after we'd finished initial pleasantries.

"Of course," Mildred agreed and bustled off. She came back carrying a cage—a large cage, containing a large, black bird. She set it down on the coffee table.

"He's a wonderful bird. Enjoyable to have around. I hate to part with him," she said and continued babbling a stream of nonsense about the wonders of the bird, which Henny and I ignored. We moved closer to the cage and saw, under and on each side of the cage door, two small holes, which once held tiny screws attaching something to the cage frame. The nameplate. Plus, the rectangular space which would have been hidden by the nameplate was a much different shade than the metal surrounding it.

"He looks like a wonderful bird," Henny said. "You're asking…?"

"Two hundred fifty dollars," Mildred replied, giving us a smile to indicate we were getting a really good deal. "He's a genuine charmer."

"Can you give us a moment?" Henny asked.

Mildred took the caged bird and disappeared. My eyes followed her from the room, and that's when I saw it. I grabbed Henny by the arm and marched him to a table holding a half dozen photos. In one of them, Doris stood smiling, her arm across the shoulders of Ashley Mae.

"I thought Mildred looked a little familiar," Henny said. "Doris's sister? What'd'ya think?"

"Sister, cousin, doesn't matter. Doris snatched the bird and brought it here. We could've figured that out without the photo, but the photo cinches it," I said.

"Let's have Doris unsnatch the bird and return it," Henny said. "Less work for us. She's coming back. Let me."

Mildred wore a big smile. "Well?"

"It's very tempting," Henny said, matching her smile. "Let me check one more time with my wife. You'll be in today and tomorrow?"

"Call me, and I'll arrange to be."

We left and headed straight to Deirdre's townhouse.

Twenty-one

Doris answered the door. Finding a lost black bird was a dream of Henny's, so I let him do the talking.

"Is Mrs. Delangersfeld in?" Henny led off.

"No, she rarely gets home any day until six or after. I would have told you if you'd called ahead."

"I think it's better we talk to you," Henny said. "The living room?"

We knew the way, and Doris followed along. Henny gestured her to a plush purple sofa. Henny and I took two plush black chairs facing it.

"Is Mildred Almodovar your sister?" Henny asked.

"I…what…?"

"We know everything. You came here Saturday when no one was home, walked out with the bird, and, I suppose, took a cab or were driven by your husband to Avenue H in Flatbush."

Doris's face elongated before my eyes. "Trapped" came the flashing headline from her eyes.

"You don't know the truth," Doris blurted, a plea for salvation rippling through her voice. "You don't know the truth."

Henny sat back and crossed his legs. He gestured for her to tell us the truth.

"You don't know what it's like here for Ashley Mae."

"Ashley Mae?" Henny asked. "What's she got to do with it?"

"Mrs. Delangersfeld has no time for the girl. She ignores her in favor of the stupid bird. She allows the bird to sit on the dining table during dinner and feeds him to keep him there. She spends the whole dinner talking to him. A bird. At the expense of her flesh and blood granddaughter, who has to sit quietly and watch this. The woman is gone all day long and talks and coos to the bird all evening. I've never seen the like. I'm more the child's grandmother than she is. Ashley Mae is a sensitive child."

I saw Henny's brow wrinkle in doubt.

"She is! I've come upon her many, many times crying her heart out, saying her grandmother loves a bird more than she loves her. It sounds ridiculous. I know it sounds ridiculous. I feel…I feel like a…a numbskull saying it, but it's the truth. I couldn't stand it any longer. I love the girl. I've taken care of her her entire life. It breaks my heart to see the way the woman ignores her. Ashley Mae thought the bird was cute, interesting, a nobody-else-she-knew-had-one kind of thing when she was three, four, five, even six. But these last few years… It's become as if Ms. Delangersfeld gave birth to a crow who gave birth to a crow. The crow was the grandchild, and Ashley Mae nothing but a pet kept in a townhouse cage."

Doris had begun to cry about three sentences back.

"So you stole the bird and gave it to your sister to sell," Henny stated.

Tears prevented a verbal answer, so Doris simply nodded.

"Did Ashley Mae know you took the bird?"

Doris gave a nasal-clearing sniff.

"I'm sure she guessed. I never told her as much, but we'd discussed many times how nice it would be around here if the bird were gone. She told me more than once, I assure you, how she hoped the bird's disappearance might make her grandmother think more about her. Maybe she was goading me to take the bird. I don't know. You see how she waited for me at the door yesterday and hugged me when I came in. I think she knows I took it, and I'm glad I did."

"We were hired to find the thief, you know."

"You're not going to have me arrested, are you? Are you? I'll get…"

Into the room Ashley Mae burst as if shot out of a cannon.

"No, no, please," she cried, tears already rolling down her cheeks. "Don't let them arrest Doris. I won't have anybody then. No, please." She threw herself down in front of Henny. "My grandmother already talks to me more. At dinner, last night she said things to me and not some old bird. She never used to. She only talked to the stupid bird before. If you let them arrest Doris, the bird will come back, and I'll be all alone again. Nobody else will take care of me like Doris does. Please, please. Don't arrest her."

Ashley Mae got to her knees and tears started dropping onto Henny's dark blue, pin-striped pants.

In a tiny voice, Ashley said, "And please don't bring Twinky back here. I'll run away if you do. Nobody will ever see me again."

Doris jumped in. "If you're concerned about the bird, I promise we won't sell Twinky to a stranger. Mildred will keep Twinky. She told me just yesterday he was good company. She likes him. He'll have a nice life. I promise. My sister will be sure of it…oh!"

"Oh, what?" Henny asked, clearly on the horns of a dilemma. I felt it, too.

"You would have been paid to bring the bird back, wouldn't you? I'll pay you. I don't have much. I don't get paid much, but I can manage a few hundred dollars."

"And I have a piggy bank. I'll give you all I have," Ashley Mae added. As soon as Ashley Mae's quavering, tiny voice struck Henny's ears, I knew the outcome. Hard-boiled, soft-hearted Henny.

"We don't want your money, Ashley Mae," he said. "Yours or Doris's. Okay, look." Henny glanced at me, and I nodded. He could do what he wanted. "Promise me Twinky stays with your sister. No stranger gets her." Henny's voice almost disappeared. "Lloyd and I will tell Ms. Delangersfeld the case is unsolvable."

"Oh, Mr. Henny," Ashley Mae cried leaping to her feet. She put her head on Henny's shoulder and wrapped her arms around him as she cried in joy.

"Hey, hey. You're schmutzing up the goods. Tears stain."

Ashley Mae lifted up her head and smiled. "I really think you look good in a shoot suit."

"Mmm, thanks."

Henny and I rose.

"Do we all understand one another?" I asked. "For the record, Henny and I weren't here today. Twinky is gone for good, but to your sister and your sister only."

Both Doris and Ashley Mae chimed in with yesses.

"Thank you so much, Mr. Henny and Lloyd," Doris said. She walked us to the door and blew us a kiss as we exited. Ashley Mae waved vigorously.

Henny and I let Gloria and Susan know the results, and the girls complimented us as two of nature's noblemen. I thanked Susan for her help, something I'd done too many times for my taste.

The following Monday afternoon, Doris and Ashley Mae paid us a visit. Ashley Mae carried a Christmas present in her hands, a rectangular box about a foot tall and six inches square.

After hellos went round, Ashley Mae said, "We're going to see the big tree in Rockefeller Center."

"You've come well out of your way," Henny pointed out.

"Ashley Mae insisted on bringing you this," Doris said.

Ashley Mae placed the gift on Henny's desk.

"Open it now," she bubbled.

Henny ripped the white wrapping paper covered with Santa faces away to reveal a cardboard box. He opened the box and lifted out a black, enameled falcon.

"I bought it with my own piggy bank money. It looks just like the one I saw on your book," Ashley Mae said excitedly. "Where's your book?"

Henny got his book from his desk and compared.

"See," Ashley Mae piped. "Same thing! I know you like them."

"She and I looked all weekend for that," Doris said, proudly.

"Grandma went away, and Doris had me all weekend. We had fun."

"Yes, we did. Okay, let's get going, sweetheart. We have another subway ride ahead of us."

"It's for both of you. You, too," Ashley Mae pointed out, not wanting to omit little old me.

I thanked her. Henny thanked her, and they left.

"What'd'ya think, Henny? Ready to get your tubes untied."

"You're hilarious," he said. "Maybe all eight-year-olds aren't devil's spawn. The jury's still out. Okay if I keep this on my desk?"

"Okay with me. Gloria's silk screen hangs on my side of the room. Fair's fair. You know," I said, "the falcon in the book was never actually found, was it?"

Henny's eyes went slowly to the statue.

"No, it wasn't. You don't think…Nah, it's impossible. But wouldn't it be nice!"

I allowed Henny to dream a while.

"We've had a pretty good run at the start of our careers, haven't we?" I said.

"We have. Me, you, and Susan."

I glared at him but, since lights and trees had begun to go up all over the city and the Christmas season was upon us, I forgave his snide remark.

"I feel good," I said.

"Me, too."

"Celebrate?"

"I don't see why not."

Henny pulled the usual bottle from his desk along with the paper cups and poured. He handed me a cup.

"To a Merry Christmas, Henny," I toasted.

"And to a prosperous New Year, Lloyd," Henny toasted.

Down the hatch went the Boone's That's All

Meet John Paulits

John Paulits lives in New York City and spent many years there teaching. He has written fiction for over thirty years, novels for children as well as adults. To learn more about John's books, visit his website: www.johnpaulits.com

Other Works from the Pen of
John Paulits

For ages 8-12

Philip Gets Even—By accident at an art show in which they are entered, Philip Felton and Emery Wyatt offend Johnny Visco, the toughest boy in sixth grade, and he promises to get even. When Johnny Visco's attacks show no sign of stopping, Philip, Emery, and Mr. Conway concoct a plan that finally puts Johnny Visco in his place and prevents him from tormenting the boys any longer.

Philip and the Case of Mistaken Identity—
Philip and his best friend Emery, detectives on the trail, try to cope with a mystifying little girl who runs them a merry chase.

The Director— The Director invites nine-year-old Tommy Whitaker to be a character in a book set in 1957. The trouble begins in the Regal movie theatre, where after the Saturday matinee. Elwood Wambo, the strange caretaker of the movie theatre, hires Tommy and his 1957 best friend, Mouse, to stay behind on future Saturdays to clean the theatre when the movie is over. The boys later learn that Wambo and his partner Jeremy are part of a gang of thieves. When their friend Smitty's bike is stolen and when Smitty himself mysteriously disappears, Tommy and his two friends, Mouse and Royal, vow to solve the mysteries of their missing friend, his missing bike...and a murder.

A Cat Tale— Hayden and his fellow cats find their way to paradise: TALULA TUPPERMAN'S HOME FOR DISTRESSED FELINES. But Rodney and Stanley, cat kidnappers, are on their trail, and suddenly cats begin to vanish. Can Hayden and his troop put a stop to these mysterious disappearances before they mysteriously vanish, too?

For ages 12-18

The Ghosts of Northwood Cemetery—When Greg Logan takes his girlfriend, Karen, on a late night walk-through of Northwood Cemetery, Karen is spooked by the silence, the darkness, and something she sees but can't explain. When they meet with two other teenagers in the cemetery, strange things begin to happen. Greg and Karen can't rest until they figure out the meaning of the strange goings-on in the Northwood Cemetery.

For ages 13-up

The Mountaintop—Jason, a seventeen-year-old Amerian, sets out for the mountaintop to determine the truth of his people's beliefs. On his journey he runs into some unexpected and eye-opening adventures. Most importantly, he meets Manda, a 17-year-old Ginder girl, who changes his life irrevocably.

For Adults

Hobson's Planet—When Culp Robinson arrives on the Hobson's Planet, he steps into a whirlwind of controversy and political upheaval. Against his will, Culp finds himself the designated savior to another planet. Having failed on Earth, he wants no part of another such quest. Now he must decide where his duty and his heart lie.

Ant-Nee's Golden Notebook— Mayhem and mix-ups follow Bruno Brunotaglia's murder of a hit man sent after him by a rival mob. Panic stricken, Bruno leaves behind a briefcase of money and an import notebook. Two down-and-out friends find the briefcase and notebook, and Bruno needs them back before his father, head of the Philly mob, blows a gasket. Will Richard get to keep the briefcase of money he found with Strangler and the Indian hard on his trail? Can Clarence make hay from the information in the notebook? It's a battle of half-wits in this deadly game of hide and seek.

Henny and Lloyd: Private Eyes—Henny and Lloyd, age mid-twenties, have completed their online course in private detecting and are now licensed PIs. They've rented an office on Centre Street in downtown NYC, a rundown apartment each in Williamsburg, Brooklyn, and now set out to make their dreams of crime-fighting come true.

The Sad Case of Brownie Terwilliger—Brownie Terwilliger looks at his opportunity of running for mayor of Philadelphia as a chance to right the wrongs of a city. He hopes to oust Milton Streezo, the incumbent, but Streezo does not take kindly to this challenge and concocts a plan to destroy Brownie, even hiring Lunky Ledbetter, famed perpetrator of dirty political tricks. Can Brownie withstand the onslaught? Will he have the opportunity to do some good in the world? Don't bet on it.

The Collected Short Stories - A man buried alive; the extinction of a gloried species; the mingling of interstellar races; a mysterious amulet; a fearful child; an animal-loving old hag; the assassination of the Almighty. Stories of horror, mystery, fantasy, and science fiction certain to raise the hairs on your neck.

The Rest is Silence—The Shakespeare Murders Vol 1 - When a body is found on the stage of the Bouwerie Lane Theatre, the AWB Theatre is thrown into turmoil, and Don Lovett, one of its actors, is suspected of murder. Can AWB actor Mark Louis exonerate his good friend and bring the life of the acting troupe back to normal?

A Dying Fall - The Shakespeare Murders Vol 2 - When the AWB Theatre Company accepts an invitation to perform on the tropical island of Illyria, they get more than they bargained for. Sudden death. Mark Louis, company member and amateur detective, suspects murder. The actors, however, must return home to New York, forcing mark to conduct his investigation a thousand miles from the crime.

To Prove a Villain - The Shakespeare Murders Vol 3 -When Mark Louis investigates the death of Kristy King's brother, what he learns upends their theatre company as well as his relationship with Kristy. Should he have let sleeping dogs lie?

A Spider Steeped—The Shakespeare Murders Vol 4 - Mark Louis and Kristy King become involved with murder when they visit Erin Blakely, a college friend of Kristy's whom she hasn't seen in half-a-dozen years. Hoping to uncover the truth about Erin's tangled life, Mark and Kristy decide to investigate four men from Erin's past and present.

A Summer Murder—Three months at the beach with friends and with a young lady named Eileen Meredith, the blonde beauty of the summer. A young woman to die for? No, a young woman to be murdered. For adults.

Henny and Lloyd's Best Cases - Henny and Lloyd, Private Eyes, solve some of the most baffling cases of their newly-launched careers.

Writing as Paul Johns:

From Out the Shadowed Night—How far would you go to achieve revenge? Brian Martin committed an unspeakable crime and managed to escape responsibility for his act. Now, sixteen years later, not only do the effects of his crime rise up out of the past, but something much more deadly begins to haunt him as well.

Prayer Preyer—Fifty years of obstacles have kept Jerry Curtis from locating Father Lockhart. Now, he's found the priest and is determined to take his revenge for the crime committed against him all those years ago.

Dear reader,

I hope you've enjoyed reading this tale of two unusual
detectives and the mysteries they solved.

Your opinion is valuable to other
readers like you,
who may be looking for books like mine.

Please consider taking a few minutes to post a review,
however brief,
on the site where you purchased this book
or on the Wings ePress web page.

You may also want to visit my author page
at the Wings' website, where you can find
all the other books in my series.

Thank you!
John Paulits

VISIT OUR WEBSITE
FOR THE FULL INVENTORY
OF QUALITY BOOKS:

www. wings-epress.com

Quality trade paperbacks and downloads
in multiple formats,
in genres ranging from light romantic comedy to
general fiction and horror. Wings has something
for every reader's taste.
Visit the website, then bookmark it.
We add new titles each month!